Bey
Clue

ond

less

LINAS ALSENAS

Amulet Books
New York

Library of Congress Cataloging-in-Publication Data

Alsenas, Linas.
Beyond clueless / by Linas Alsenas.
pages cm
Summary: Fourteen-year-old Marty Sullivan attends an all-girl Catholic high school while her best friend, Jimmy, goes to public school in a different town and when he comes out of the closet, he finds a new group of friends while Marty finds connections— and also confusion and uncertainty—through her school's fall musical.
ISBN 978-1-4197-1496-2 (hardback)
[1. Interpersonal relations—Fiction. 2. Catholic schools—Fiction. 3. High schools—Fiction. 4. Schools—Fiction. 5. Gays—Fiction. 6. Coming out (sexual orientation)—Fiction. 7. Theater—Fiction. 8. Musicals—Fiction.] I. Title.
PZ7.A46264Bey 2015
[Fic]—dc23
2015005780

Printed and bound in USA
10 9 8 7 6 5 4 3 2 1

Amulet Books are available at special discounts when purchased in quantity for premiums and promotions as well as fundraising or educational use. Special editions can also be created to specification. For details, contact specialsales@abramsbooks.com or the address below.

THE ART OF BOOKS SINCE 1949
115 West 18th Street
New York, NY 10011
www.abramsbooks.com

FOR BERT

artha. Wake up!"

My eyelids pressed down hard onto my eyeballs, feeling like lead blankets at an X-ray. Slowly I managed to pry the lids open.

Derek's face, full of concern, hovered above me.

"Wh-wh-what's—" I stammered.

He shushed me. "It's OK, it's OK. You fainted."

I was having trouble focusing. Fainted . . . fainted. Me? I fainted?

Inside my skull, it felt like my brain was expanding, pushing against my ears in the same rhythm as my heartbeat. I turned my head left to look around the room, and—

Urinals?

Reality came rushing back at me, at full force. I suddenly understood that my head was resting on the gross tile floor of the men's bathroom. I gasped, struggling for air, despite the sharp smell of disinfectant. About two feet away from my face was a moist clump of dust, dirt, and hair that shivered with my every breath.

Eww.

Do not hurl, Marty. Do not hurl . . . again.

I turned back to look at the ceiling. Then I slowly became

aware that I was crying, makeup streaking across my face and pooling in my ears.

Basically, I was a hot mess.

It wasn't just the throwing up and the fainting. In the past half hour I had literally *stumbled* across a series of insane surprises that still sent my brain into a tailspin.

Ohhh. Oh, yes. It was all coming back to me now. And all my friends hated me.

I think it's pretty safe to say that *this*, this moment here, was a truly low point for me. And on this, the most terrible day of my life, I just could not understand: How had I ever gotten here?

What had I ever done to deserve all this?

Well, for the sake of context, I guess the most logical place to start is at the very, *very* beginning, four years ago, at Chippewa Elementary, where I met Jimmy Caradonna in fifth-grade phys ed. There are three different classes within the grade, but they had to combine two classes at a time for phys ed because the gym was also the cafeteria, and there weren't enough periods in the day to let every class in the school have its own gym period.

So, imagine fifty eleven-year-olds going nuts playing kickball. Horrific, isn't it? Well, at least that's how Jimmy and I felt about it, and for some reason we were the only ones who did. Everyone else thought kickball was God's greatest gift to humanity. I kid you not, there would be rumors about whether we'd play kickball later in the day. And if we ended up doing ring toss or relays or whatever instead, kids would actually get their parents to call the school to complain. I'm not lying. Really.

OK, so there's me and Jimmy, trying to lie as low as possible while our classmates worked out whatever deep-seated aggressions they had on a purple rubber ball. We were always picked last, of course—not because we were the worst athletes, but because the team captains were always afraid that our attitudes would infect the rest of the teams' spirit and, therefore, oh, my *God*, cause them to lose.

But since we were always the last ones picked, Jimmy and I were never on the same team. We had never spoken to each other before—Jimmy had moved to Bracksville from Michigan at the beginning of the year—but as the only Kickball Infidels, we obviously each knew who the other was. He was the skinny kid with short black hair and really blue eyes, and I was the blond dork who was obsessed with musicals, especially *Rent* and *Assassins* at the time.

But after all the fifth graders were required to learn the American Sign Language alphabet during Difficulty Appreciation Week, Jimmy and I started commiserating across the kickball diamond by sneaking hand gestures. When one of the team captains caught on to what we were doing, she complained to the teacher that we were plotting to ruin the game. Then Jimmy communicated his feelings toward the captain in a different kind of sign language—and got us both sent to the principal's office.

We've been inseparable ever since.

Well, sort of. Until a few months ago. Which, by the way, was after four blissful years of best-friendship. Dozens of slumber parties, hundreds of nicknames, and thousands of inside jokes later, Jimmy, like all normal human beings in Bracksville, started school at Bracksville High. I, on the other hand, was shipped off to Our Lady of the Oaks School for Girls. Yup: Oaks. Girls. Our Lady of. No, this is *not* 1953, as the name might suggest, but the school definitely still thinks it is.

You see, my family is Catholic, and my parents both went to Catholic schools, so they "firmly believe, based on experience, that a single-sex high school education in a Catholic setting is the most fertile ground for a budding intellect that [they] can provide." Did you get that? Single-sex. Fertile budding. Needless to say, I wasn't going to submit to the malicious will of two religious zealots without a struggle. But after a number of shrieking fights, two hunger strikes, and more than a few calls to Social Services later, I was forced to accept the tragic reality that every fourteen-year-old in this land of so-called freedom has, in fact, none. I was going to Our Lady of the Oaks, and there was nothing I could do about it.

So the end of last year was a time of tearful good-byes, hysterically scribbled yearbook notes, and desperate promises to keep in touch. OK, maybe I took it a little far—most people assumed I was getting shipped off to a Romanian orphanage or something. But the pain of separation was real: I was like a monarch butterfly about to be pinned to a musty old corkboard. A musty old corkboard called Our Lady of the Freakin' Oaks.

Let me give you a visual, just so you understand the true depths of my suffering. To get to Our Lady from Bracksville, you have to drive twenty-five minutes *in the opposite direction* of the city. Mind you, Bracksville is already a thirty-minute commute to Cleveland—you do the math. The school itself is on about two acres in the middle of millions of acres of corn. Not the pretty rolling hills of corn on the labels of vegetable shortening, but the flat, dry, cricket-ridden cornfields of Ohio. Field of dreams this was not. In fact, when the school was built in the mid-1950s in that oh-so-pretty style of beige brick and turquoise metal panels, they realized how sadly ironic Our Lady of the Oaks would be without any trees. So they planted about fifty oaks around the lot. Thanks to some fungus that causes "oak wilt," there is now one remaining oak that gets sprayed down with DDT (or something equally deadly) once a week by Sister Joan. And, thanks to the fact that it's the tallest thing around for miles, it has become the county lightning rod, which means there are only about seven leaves left on the poor thing.

This is where my parents believed I would find fertile ground.

OK, so maybe there is *one* redeeming thing about the school. About ten years ago, one of its alumnae died and left a ton of money to the school—her family fortune had come from a certain well-known floor wax. She had earmarked the money to be used for a theater, which would be named after her, Maureen Jerry. The amount of money she left was clearly more than the school had ever seen, because Jerry Hall is by far the nicest part of campus. (Completely coincidentally, Jerry Hall is also the name of rocker Mick Jagger's second wife.)

The building is actually kind of amazing. It has fly space for at least ten different backdrops (who would ever need more than five in any one show?), and the stage is forty feet across and fifty feet deep—with, like, sixteen trapdoors! Also, the dressing room has a snack machine with Twix bars.

Speaking. Of. Which. I love Twix bars. I mean, I am *completely* obsessed with them. If the Mars candy company ever needs someone to pledge their eternal, undying love for them in a commercial, I am so there. Twix bars are truly— oh, words fail me—ambrosia from the gods! Manna from the heavens! I've already written Mars, Inc., more than a few letters over the years, volunteering my services, but still, if you ever hear they are looking for someone . . .

Sorry, I'm getting way off track. Where was I? Oh, yeah, so Jimmy's settling into life at Bracksville, while I'm in rural exile. We made a pact that we would see each other at least every other day, no matter what. That lasted about five minutes after school began, until we realized how much work high school was going to be. Don't get me started on the crazy craploads of homework I get at Our Dear Lady. I swear to God I'm going to die from sleep deprivation, and still we're supposed to be involved in every extracurricular activity under the sun or we won't get into college and we'll end up living with our parents and working at Pizza Hut for fifteen years until we finally drink a bottle of bleach to end the misery into which our lives have devolved. But I said I wouldn't get started, so I won't.

Anyway, our weekends became that much more important.

Then Jimmy met Derek.

The End.

ine, yes, there's a lot more to it than that; still, it *was* the
end of an era.

One day, only a few days after school began, Jimmy called
me up, all serious, saying, "We have to talk. You need to
come over." This was very un-Jimmy-like speech. Normally,
every conversation with him starts off with a scream—like,
a happy scream. Then we proceed to the salutation, which
usually involves calling the other person a fetching vegetable or fruit, like "you ravishing radish" or "my saucy persim-
mon." So this was bad. Real bad.

Of course, I immediately assumed that he had brain
cancer. Or, worse, that he was moving back to Michigan.

I threw on a hoodie and headed over to Jimmy's house.
He lives on Cottonwood Drive, and I live on Iroquois Trail,
both of which are cul-de-sac streets in their own develop-
ments. In sixth grade, there was this one day when we were
playing with his dad's iPad. We tagged our houses on a satellite overview of the area. Seriously, it was like fireworks
went off in our brains. We lived *way closer* than we'd ever
realized! The forest behind my house was the *same one* that
was behind his; we just had to work out a trail, using the
iPad and a roll of pink ribbon, tying bows on trees along the

way. So, instead of a twenty-minute-long bike ride, it was just a ten-minute hike through the woods. Best day ever.

On the serious-conversation day, however, the ribbons had long since faded to gray. But whatever, even if they had fallen off, it's not like I didn't know the trail without them, and I arrived at Jimmy's house in no time. He led me up to his room, all ashen and nervous, and made me sit on his bed.

"Here, take this," he said, handing me a Twix bar. You know, like I'm some sort of zoo animal. Here, little monkey, take the pretty candy! Obviously I didn't open it. I was afraid it contained sedatives or something. This was all very freaky. Freaky, freaky, freaky.

"Martha," he said, "I have something to tell you. About me. It's . . . it's rather personal."

And apparently "rather" formal, I thought. This whole time, Jimmy was sweating like he was doing downward-facing dog in Bikram Yoga or something. I started developing a new theory that maybe it wasn't cancer. Maybe, instead, Jimmy's chest would open up, and an alien baby would spring out to attack me. I fingered the strap on my book bag. Bring it on, little alien.

"I'm . . . well, I think I'm . . ." Big pause.

"Yeeesss?"

"I'm . . ."

An alien? A cannibal? Ryan Gosling's love child?

"Holy bejeezus, Jimmy, what the hell?"

He winced. "OK, OK, hold on—I need a drink."

He got up and grabbed an iced tea from his mini-fridge. He kept one eye trained on me as his Adam's apple bobbed with every gulp. I twisted a lock of blond hair, wrapping it around the end of my index finger.

Finally, Jimmy regained some shred of composure, but of course by now it was clear that this announcement involved some kind of family drama. His parents were divorcing? Something with his little sister? Jimmy and I were pretty much never serious about anything, so I wasn't sure how to handle a conversation like that.

My finger pulsed, and I realized I had wrapped my hair around it way too tightly.

Jimmy opened and closed his mouth a few times—false starts.

Then suddenly he spat out,

"Imetsomeone.

"IthinkmaybeImaylikethissomeone.

"Thissomeoneisaguy.

"I'mnotsurebutIthinkImightbegay."

Uh, excuse me? I stared at him. Did I hear that right? Did he just say he thinks he's gay?

Jimmy stared back at me, those blue eyes looking like Bambi's watching his mother die.

"Uh . . . and?" I said.

Jimmy's shoulders slumped. "What do you mean, 'and'? I just told you I'm gay."

"Well, of course you are. I've figured that since we were about ten."

"But now it's true."

"I know!" What was I supposed to say? "Oh, my God! I had no idea"? But for some reason, Jimmy was getting mad.

"What do you mean, you *know*? How could you possibly know? You're not me!"

"Jimmy, you're the gayest kid I know. I mean, take a look around you: This isn't exactly butch." His eyes scanned the vintage fringed lampshade, the wall color he'd spent weeks trying to decide on ("Verona Green"), and the framed One Direction poster (the original five) over his bed.

"I . . . like baseball!" he countered, which merely got a snort-chuckle in response. "Anyway, that's not the point," he continued. "We're friends, and you were supposed to believe me when I told you before that I didn't *know* if I was gay. You don't just draw your own conclusions and then *pretend* to believe me!"

Oh, great. Now he was in full self-righteous-indignation mode.

"So I'm supposed to completely ignore reality?" I asked. "Last time I checked, friendship is not the same thing as forced stupidity."

"No, but while you were checking, did it say friendship meant lying?"

"I was not *lying*."

"You were totally lying!"

"Well, so were you!"

"I was not."

"Oh, *please*, everyone always knew you were gay. Including you, princess."

We glared at each other for a full five seconds.

"Homophobe," he said.

I snorted in response. "Delusional freak."

Another glare. But then, ten seconds later, I couldn't help it: I started to crack a smile. Then it broadened. Jimmy's glare held out for another few seconds, but then we both started giggling, erupting finally into a release of laughter. I don't know what it is about the two of us, but just looking at each other makes us lose our shit. That's usually all it takes, and something clicks, and we're back to normal.

"Come on, Jimmy, don't make me laugh this hard. Now I have to go pee. But when I come back, I want the full report on this mysterious new stranger recruiting you to be a homosexual."

Jimmy threw a pillow at me, but I'd already closed the door behind me.

So it turns out that with the start of a new academic year at a new school, our little Jimmy had decided it was time for some self-discovery. He took the bus into the city to check out a certain notorious gay hot spot in University Circle. I mean, this little café is actually pretty unremarkable: It has fluorescent-colored walls painted in a flower-power motif, a few comfy flea-market couches, a collection of mismatched metal, plastic, and wooden tables and chairs. But it was known for being gay-friendly, so from the way people would talk about it, you'd imagine it was Sodom and Gomorrah, or Amsterdam's red-light district, or, I dunno, some sort of sex-crazed fever dream.

Jimmy walked by the café about six times, trying his hardest to look like he was on his way somewhere *impor-tant*, that he just *happened* to be traversing the same block every two-point-three minutes. Finally he managed to gather enough chutzpah to walk in—and immediately made a beeline to the counter to order without looking around. You know, like he was actually there for the jasmine tea.

Five minutes later, he had settled into one of the comfy couches and, at last, started breathing again. Of course, he was also pretending to read his copy of *The Age of Inno-cence* with a muscular intensity to avoid making eye contact with all the Gays around him (who had long ago stopped pretending to read). Then, a certain handsome fellow—later to be identified as Derek—sat down beside him and started coughing. And by "coughing" I mean "deep, phlegm-gargling hacking." Apparently, Derek really was mostly there for the tea. How that boy managed to get bronchitis in late August continues to be a mystery.

Serendipitously, Jimmy feels the same way about Halls cough drops that I do about Twix bars—except that, tragi-cally, because of its quasi-medicinal status, he can't respon-sibly succumb to the same level of indulgence that I can. But he always carries cough drops around, just in case his throat gets scratchy. Which, amazingly, happens several times a day! (When Jimmy gets a cold, he practically throws a party.)

So a cough drop, an awkward explanation, and a con-versation later, Jimmy shed the last vestiges of his heterosexual delusion and decided that this Derek character was the cat's pajamas.

"Well, good for you!" I told Jimmy, stretching out on his bed. "Do you have any visuals?"

A slow smile made its way across Jimmy's face, despite his best efforts to stop it.

"You do! Lemme see!"

"You can't laugh," Jimmy insisted.

"I would never!"

"Oh, please. You've refined making fun of *me* into its own sophisticated art form," Jimmy grumbled, but he made his way to the computer, anyway. "OK, he has a profile, but the pic he posted really doesn't do him justice."

In no time, I was looking at a devilishly good-looking, chiseled-jawed boy.

That's when I felt a searing flash of envy go through me— lonely, loveless me. You know, it's funny. Until that moment I never really thought I was missing something. But now I felt a strange, hollow sensation, perhaps of being left behind.

"Yummy. Is he Indian?"

"His parents are from Sri Lanka."

I scanned Derek's "favorites": *Catcher in the Rye*, juggling, Cape Cod, postcards, blah, blah, blah.

"Huh. He certainly has an earnest profile, but does he have a sense of humor?" I caught myself: Marty, don't be a bitch. "I mean, I'm not criticizing. You just can't really tell from this."

Jimmy squirmed a little. "Well . . . I wouldn't say he's Jimmy Fallon or anything, but he has a funny dark side that no one sees until they really get to know him. Like, snarky."

All of a sudden I was seized with the desire to leave. I straightened up and picked up my book bag. "Well, you *know* I like a good snark. A very promising fellow." I patted Jimmy's shoulder. "But now, my succulent squash, I, alas, must take my leave. I have my first algebra test on Friday and a drama club meeting tomorrow night, so I have to study tonight. When do I get to meet this Derek person?"

"Actually, you can meet him on Friday! He's coming over. We're going to watch bad sitcoms and eat cookie dough. It'll be fun! We can celebrate your algebraic success."

I felt another stab in my chest. That would have been really fun—if it had been just us.

"Super. Sounds awesome."

I speed-walked home the long way, via the sidewalks, lost in thought over this new Derek development. Jimmy and I barely had any time to spend together as it was, and if he all of a sudden had a boyfriend, where would I fit in? What if I despised Derek after I met him? If push came to shove, whom would Jimmy choose?

I stared hard at the pavement, my hands clenched into fists around my book-bag straps.

For so long, it had always been Jimmy and Marty. Jimmy and Marty everything. School, shopping, weekends, TV-watching, late-night snarfing of cough drops and Twix bars—we did everything together. He got the meanings of all my jokes, all my pointed looks, all my thoughts—honestly, I usually didn't even have to say anything, and he'd totally know what I was thinking.

But now, high school was a totally different story. Now it was Just Me at this new school with all these other girls. I mean, they were pretty nice so far, a few days in—it's not like they had been mean to me or anything like that—but I hadn't really *connected* with anyone there. Most girls already had friends at Oaks from whatever Catholic elementary school they'd gone to, so to them I was this odd satellite just outside their orbits, passing by. They seemed fine and pleasant, but I needed someone on my wavelength, someone who really *understood* me.

Before tonight I could take comfort in the fact that Jimmy was in the same boat as me, missing me at his new school. But now I wasn't so sure. He had this whole Derek thing to look forward to, to obsess about, to define himself by, even though Derek didn't go to his school. He was becoming Jimmy without Marty. But who was Marty without Jimmy?

Aaaargh. And what was wrong with me—why couldn't I have met *my* Derek first? At this rate, I was never going to meet a Derek. Not too many Dereks roaming the estrogen-soaked halls of Our Lady. Should I just accept reality and get my name legally changed to Third Wheel Sullivan?

iss Sullivan. Earth to Martha."

I looked up to see Mr. Dartagnan knocking on the whiteboard, eyebrows raised.

"Uh-huh?"

"Can you tell us what the cubic root of twenty-seven is, please?"

My brain hadn't caught up with my face, which by now looked *very* interested in everything Mr. Dartagnan had to say.

"Uh, sure." Out of the corner of my eye, I saw someone holding up three fingers under the next desk. "It's three."

"Correct." Mr. Dartagnan frowned, clearly disappointed that I had gotten it right. He turned back to the board. "So, if we take that cubic root and subtract it from this dividend . . ."

Those three fingers belonged to the Asian girl with the weird name, which I couldn't remember for the life of me. It had only been about a week since school had started, and I had a hard enough time sorting out all the Kellys, Jens, and Megans, let alone some name that started with an *X*. I gave her a smile of thanks, and she smiled back quickly and looked down at her math book.

After class I saw X Girl sitting by herself in the lunch-room. For the past week the social seating situation had been very random. On the first day I had thought that there would be a clear social hierarchy mapped out by where people sat in the cafeteria. I mean, anyone who's ever seen a high school movie knows that. But as it turned out, people kept mixing it up every day, so it didn't seem weird just to plop down anywhere to eat. I suppose it's hard to develop patterns when you have a different class schedule every day, and maybe things were different at an all-girls school—or maybe it was too early in the year for people to define power relationships. Well, whatever the reason, I thought, hopefully it'll stay that way. I placed my lunch down across the table from X Girl.

"Hey, do you mind if I sit with you?" I asked.

She looked up and shook her head. I decided then and there that this cute, small, shy, smart girl was nothing less than Adorable. She even had little butterfly barrettes in her hair. Aww . . .

"Thanks for helping me out in class. You must be really good at math," I said.

Her face suddenly darkened. "Why, because I'm Asian?"

Uh—or maybe not so cute. Blood rushed to my face. I was dumbfounded.

But then she smiled. "I'm kidding. Relax. Hey, I'm Xiang." She pronounced it *Seng*.

It took me a moment to process, but I managed an uneasy grin.

"Martha. Well, Marty."

"Actually, I really hate math. I just knew the answer to that one."

"Oh, well, thanks again." I fished out my pumpkin-seed-butter-and-banana sandwich and reviewed the rest of my lunch. Great, thanks, Dad. I was just craving these carrot sticks that always dry out and warp by lunchtime. Having two health nuts for parents sucked royally. Even the juice box was actually soy milk—like the fructose in real juice would make me diabetic or something. (Actually, I kinda like soy milk, but you see what I'm saying.)

"Have you heard the rumor that Mr. Dartagnan's name is actually Mr. Darton, but he changed it to make himself seem more fancy? Major insecurity issues." I thought it was a pretty dumb rumor, but I couldn't think of anything else to say.

Xiang smiled. "Ooooh, that'll give me something fun to mull over in class. Have you noticed that his socks have his initials on them?"

"Really?" I giggled. "So they don't get mixed up with the other campers' socks?"

"They're actually embroidered that way. That's a lot of attention to give a sock, if you ask me." Xiang nibbled on an apple slice.

"Well, I hope he's grateful that he doesn't have to wear these plaid skirts. I never had to deal with gross men leering at me until I got this uniform. How, exactly, does this uniform encourage Catholic morals?"

Xiang gave a sly smile. "Priestly morals, perhaps."

My, my, this Xiang girl was quite the spitfire, wasn't she? Jimmy would definitely like her.

Oh—Jimmy. My mood dimmed a bit as I pictured Jimmy eating lunch at Bracksville High. Whom did he eat lunch with? Fred, the gamer guy? Big Amy? Or someone I didn't know, from some other middle school?

Xiang studied me for a moment. "So I take it you didn't go to Catholic grade school."

"No, the public elementary school in my town. You?"

"Homeschooled." My eyes widened, and she continued. "It took me three years to convince my parents to send me to a real school so that I could learn normal socialization skills. And they only agreed to this place because it's all girls, run by nuns, and in the middle of nowhere. You have no idea what a relief it is to be out of that house." She wiped her mouth with a napkin.

"No way! I had the exact opposite experience. On the first day of school my parents literally had to use a bolt cutter when I chained myself to my bed. I *definitely* didn't want to come here."

Xiang started to giggle but cut it off when she realized I maybe wasn't kidding.

"All my friends go to Bracksville High," I added sadly.

"Really? I live in Bracksville! Wilton Road."

"No way! I live on Iroquois! I thought I knew everyone our age in town. Your parents really kept you under wraps, didn't they?"

She rolled her eyes. "You have no idea. My house should be registered as a Chinese consulate. The only time I met other 'American' kids was at Cleveland Youth Orchestra." She brightened up. "Hey, we should carpool! Both my parents usually have to stay late at work on Thursdays, so we haven't quite figured out how to get me home. These past two weeks I had to ask my cousin to pick me up, and his car smells like warm tuna salad."

"Yeesh. OK. I'll ask my mom!"

Did I just make a friend? I know this sounds *incredibly* cheesy, but as I walked out of the lunchroom that day, I suddenly felt a little bit . . . taller. It had been a long time since I'd met a new friend—Jimmy had filled up the whole "friend" category for the past few years, and before that I guess I was too young to actually notice it happening. Part of me wanted to stop this whole Xiang thing now. I mean, I felt like I was cheating on my friendship with Jimmy. But on the other hand, if Jimmy was out finding a boyfriend and eating lunch with God-knows-who, he was already abandoning our BFF relationship.

Oh, Lord, what was I thinking? *Relationship?* Clearly, I had to get over these dependency issues with Jimmy. It's true that Xiang was no Jimmy—Jimmy and I basically shared a brain, we were so in sync—but beggars can't be choosers. With Jimmy charging ahead with his own life, I had to start leading mine.

Just then, I noticed a brightly colored poster hanging in the hallway.

DRAMA CLUB MEETING TODAY, SEPT. 3!!

COME FIND OUT WHAT THIS YEAR'S FALL MUSICAL WILL BE—

AND HOW TO BE IN IT!

3:00 P.M., JERRY HALL

My life so far has revolved around two loves: Jimmy and theater.

Well, at least I've got one left.

After school that day, I found Xiang by her locker.

"Hey, I was wondering if you wanted to go to the drama club meeting with me."

Then, immediately after I said it, I realized that the invitation was probably too much, too soon. I mean, we just had our first real conversation a few hours ago. I didn't want to seem like a stalker or anything.

Fortunately, Xiang didn't seem fazed by my smothering of her.

"Yeah, I would, but I can't act," she said, packing books into her bag. "And I definitely don't sing."

"Well, there are tons of other things you could do," I said. "You could be a stage manager, props coordinator, a costume designer . . ."

Xiang rolled her eyes.

". . . or, you know, you could go straight home instead."

Xiang hesitated. I smiled more broadly.

"You're a special kind of evil, you know," she finally said.

"Yup."

"I'm telling you right now: Don't expect me to do any acting or singing or tap-dancing shit."

Yikes. "Understood."

Just before the door slammed on Xiang's locker, I spotted a box of cigarettes inside.

"What?" asked Xiang, because I clearly failed to hide my surprise.

"Oh. Um, nothing."

Cigarettes? Who *was* this person? Instead of making me feel older, high school was making me feel very, very young.

Oh, well, no time to dwell on that now.

The drama club meeting was being held at Jerry Hall. I figured that there would be—what?—twenty people there for a drama club meeting? Maybe thirty, forty? I mean, only about seven hundred students go to Our Lady. But when we walked into the theater, I almost died. There must have been at least a hundred and fifty people there, almost filling the entire auditorium. Was drama really that popular here because of Jerry Hall? How was I ever going to get a part?

Xiang turned to me, asking, "Are you sure this is the right place?"

I shrugged, and we took two seats in the back.

A very small, very old nun was onstage, trying to turn on a microphone. She banged it on her knee, and a piercing scream of feedback shot through the theater, immediately silencing the crowded assembly.

"Bingo," she said, chuckling to herself. She patted down the front of her skirt, then looked out across the sea of students.

"Welcome to the fall musical introductory meeting. My name is Sister Mary Alice. I've been directing the musicals here for the past thirteen years."

Xiang muttered loudly, "Since she was, like, eighty-five years old?" I slid down in my seat, hoping no one had overheard her. Xiang was quickly going from Potential Friend to Total Liability.

Sister Mary Alice continued. "As I'm sure many of you are aware, the Our Lady of the Oaks Drama Club stages two major productions every year, the fall musical and the spring play. I'm delighted to see so many of you expressing interest in the former." She gave us all a stern look. "Out of pure love for the theater, I'm sure." There was low-level giggling throughout the audience, and Xiang and I exchanged bewildered looks.

The nun continued in her warbly voice. "Now. First things first. I know you are all eager to hear which musical we will be presenting this year. Let me assure you, it wasn't an easy decision after all your suggestions from last year, and the board has really gone out on a limb to approve this choice. But I'm sure we are up to the challenge."

Sister Mary Alice took a moment to cough lightly. She cleared her throat and patted her chest while one hundred and fifty some girls leaned forward in their seats. This woman sure knows her drama, I thought to myself.

"The musical for this season will be . . . drumroll? *The Sound of Music*."

There was silence. Then a collective slumping of shoulders. I could practically hear the blood draining from everyone's faces. *The Sound of Music*? So we were going to be either nuns or bratty Austrian children? What teenager wants to sing "Do-Re-Mi" in front of an audience?

25

A low, angry murmur began to grow. Sister Mary Alice's hand flew to her mouth, and she started bouncing. It took me a moment to realize she was laughing.

"I'm just kidding, girls! Just kidding!" she cried, still bouncing. "It's not *The Sound of Music*. It's Stephen Sondheim's *Into the Woods*."

I've never seen a group of people so relieved before. Xiang turned to me, her eyes bright and flashing. "That was *hilarious*. Amazing. You know, I'm actually starting to like this lady . . ." She settled back into her seat, looking the happiest I'd seen her yet.

Sister Mary Alice wiped tears from her eyes with the palm of one hand and let out a "Whooo!"

My brain started going through the show's characters while Sister Mary Alice continued. Rapunzel, the Witch, the evil Stepmother, the Baker's Wife . . .

"I imagine most of you are familiar with this musical because of the recent Hollywood film adaptation. Written by Stephen Sondheim and James Lapine, the show premiered on Broadway in 1987. The musical uses familiar characters and stories from fairy tales to analyze a multitude of themes, such as community, responsibility, adulthood, family, love . . . and even sex." She waited for the inevitable tittering to die down after the last word. She took a deep breath and became very serious.

"I'm going to be honest with you. This is a very, very complicated and mature piece—dramatically, musically, technically, conceptually—you name it. It is not a typical show for a high school production, especially because of its adult themes. It's a dark show about bad choices. So I wasn't kidding when I said the board was taking a huge risk this year."

No one moved a muscle.

Sister Mary Alice looked out at the audience with smiling eyes.

"But if I am certain of anything, it is *you*. Great women, such as yourselves, will rise to the challenge and be *luminous*."

I felt goose bumps. I admit it, I did.

"Now, I like nuns as much as anybody"—(insert heartfelt laughter here)—"but I'm not sure shows like that are interesting for you. At least, that's what I gather from your show suggestions every year. Musical theater is art, and art should challenge us, excite us, make our hearts pump a little bit, make our brains spin. And I look forward to our achieving that together this fall." She positively beamed at us.

"Now. Back to business. First, please note that the performances will be on November thirteenth and fourteenth. This is pretty self-evident, but if you know you can't make those dates, please don't waste everyone's time by auditioning. Also, I've selected Jenny McCafferty as the stage manager. Many of you may remember her for her extraordinary work managing the spring play, when she was just a sophomore."

A tall blond girl in the front row shot up from her seat and turned around, giving a sweeping arm wave to the audience. This was clearly her red-carpet moment, and I could feel Xiang shuddering next to me with suppressed laughter. Clutching a plastic clipboard to her chest, Jenny marched up the stage steps and grabbed the microphone from poor Sister Mary Alice.

"Thank you, Sister. Hey, ladies, let's hear it for the fall musical!"

Dead silence. How awkward.

Unperturbed, Jenny kept going. "Yeah! All right! This year's musical is going to be a big one, so I'm going to be selecting *two* assistant stage managers to help me in coordinating everything. Each of these positions is going to be *really important*, and I'm going to be *very selective* in choosing the individuals to fill them. Please submit applications to me at my e-mail address, which you can find in the directory. Remember, it's m-c-c-a-f-f-e-r-t-y—not m-*a*-c-c-a-f-f-e-r-t-y. I will be holding personal interviews in the next few days, as there's gonna be *a lot* of preparatory work to be done before the auditions next Wednesday."

Xiang turned to me and whispered, "Well, so much for that. If you think I'm going to deal with Miss McBossypants down there, you've got another think coming."

"Don't worry," I replied, "we'll figure something out . . ."

Sister Mary Alice clawed at Jenny's hands for the microphone and finally managed to yank it away. With a strained smile, Sister said, "Thank you, Jenny. As Miss McCafferty mentioned, we have set the date for auditions: September ninth. Please come prepared with a short monologue and a song—with or without piano sheet music. There are eighteen roles in the play. Twelve roles for women, and six"—Sister gave us that hard look again—"for men. So, tell your friends at other schools."

Xiang and I looked at each other in simultaneous comprehension. Ohhhhhhh, so *that's* why there were so many people interested in drama club.

Boys.

"Ugh, another week finally over!"

I heaved my monster book bag onto the kitchen counter. Damn textbooks. Or, more accurately, damn weekend homework.

My mother gave me a quick, annoyed look from her desk and went back to coding invoices—or whatever it is she does all day. My mom's some sort of "freelance accountant"—actually, I'm not sure *what* she does, exactly; for all I know, she runs the World Bank. Lots of paper, lots of numbers, and her hand usually looks like a blur over the calculator. But she gets to work from home a lot, which I guess she likes. Frankly, I don't see how she does it—if *I* worked from home, there would be plenty of talk shows and soaps going on, not tax forms and spreadsheets.

I poured myself a glass of orange juice and started rummaging through the cupboards. Dried apricots, dehydrated veggie mix, some sort of organic nut bar . . .

"Geez, why don't we have any *normal* snacks, like crackers or chips or pretzels or anything that any *normal* person would consider eating?" I reluctantly grabbed a snack-pack of yogurt-covered raisins.

My mother peered at me over her reading glasses. "Don't

eat too much. Your father's going to start making dinner soon. I think he said something about lasagna."

"Ooooh, let me guess: a chopped-walnut-and-mushroom filling with pressed organic heirloom tomato sauce, covered with whole-wheat pasta, and smothered in goat cheese. Oh, and sprinkled with freshly chopped wheatgrass. Can't wait." I pretended to stick a finger down my throat and made gagging noises.

"Marty, you don't know how good you have it. Not everyone gets to eat as healthfully as you do."

My parents looooove vegetables, which makes it really easy for them to eat a lot of crazy-healthy food. Like, they're *obsessed* with them. The stranger and weirder the variety, the better. (Which, by the way, has been helpful in coming up with greetings for Jimmy.)

"What good is health food if you can't swallow it?"

My mother just rolled her eyes and shuffled a stack of papers.

"Your father is very gung-ho about seeing some movie tonight. I think it's a Hitchcock."

I shook my head. "Nope. I'm going over to Jimmy's. We're going to sniff glue or something. Maybe spray-paint obscenities all over the playground at Chippewa."

"As long as you don't get caught," she said blandly.

"Knock on wood."

Two hours later, I *was* knocking on wood—the front door to the Caradonna home. It was dark already, but I carry a mini-flashlight on my key chain to make it through the shortcut in the forest. I mean, the woods aren't *that* big; they're just kind of long, so at any point you can make out lights from houses through the trees. But still, you don't want to step on a sleeping deer or something.

Not that I've ever heard of anyone doing that; it's just something that seems totally plausible.

Doesn't it?

OK, moving on.

Jimmy's little sister, Jeanie, answered. She is officially the weirdest nine-year-old on the planet. She was wearing a black robe of some sort and had black mascara all over her face.

"Um, hi, Jeanie. What's up?"

"Welcome to the House of Despair," she hissed.

"Um, okee-dokee, thanks. I'm here to see Jimmy."

"Oh, what does it matter? We're all going to die." She wandered off, leaving me standing there with the door open.

"Right. OK, I'll find him. Don't worry about it," I called after her. I started up the stairs but stopped when I heard Jimmy's voice down in the living room. I spun around but then froze again a second later when I heard a bunch of guys laughing. Like, not two guys. More like . . . four or five. What happened to cookie dough, me, Jimmy, and his new boyfriend? Who were these people?

I peeked through the doorway and saw Jimmy sprawled on the couch next to Derek, who looked just like his profile pic. Very cute. Then there was a redheaded guy on the floor wearing a Green Lantern T-shirt (hmm, I figured about a 6.5 on a 10-point scale in the looks department) and a dark-haired dude in the recliner (who was hard to rate, since his face was barely visible under his baseball cap).

"Uh . . . hi."

"Marty!" Jimmy's face lit up like a bare bulb. "Hey, guys, this is Marty, like I was telling you about."

They all stared at me.

Jimmy jumped up. "Marty, this is Kirby"—Green Lantern gave me a nod—"and this is Oliver. And *this* is Derek."

Derek was up on his feet and presenting me his hand. Like, for a handshake? What was this, a diplomatic summit?

"Hey, nice to meet you," I said cautiously, letting my hand get pumped.

"Jimmy's told me *so* much about you—I mean, he's *always* talking about you. Great to meet you, just *great*."

He was so intense, I could only smile weakly and nod in response. Later on, Jimmy would tell me that Derek was only behaving that way because he was reeeeally nervous about meeting me, Jimmy's best friend. I turned to Jimmy, giving him my who-the-hell-are-these-other-dudes? look.

"Oh, um, Kirby and Oliver go to school with Derek in Weeksburg. They met in the GSA."

I was at a loss. "What's that, like a division of Homeland Security or something?"

They all laughed. Kirby threw some popcorn at Oliver, saying, "Yeah, we're spies!"

"As if you could keep *anything* a secret," Oliver shot back.

Kirby raised an eyebrow. "Sweetheart, you have no *idea* what a trove of secrets I keep."

Jimmy pulled me and Derek onto the couch so that he was between us. "Martha goes to a Catholic girls' school, so I don't think they have a Gay-Straight Alliance there."

Ohhh, gay club. Right.

Kirby smirked. "What about all the dykes? I mean, come on, there's got to be a lot of that going on at an *all-girls* school."

I shrugged. Honestly, it had never even occurred to me that some of the students at Our Lady were gay. "Um, I have no idea, actually. I think maybe the conservative Catholic parents would get freaked out if there were some sort of club. Or the nuns would get fired by the Pope or something. Anyway, I haven't met any lesbians," I waffled.

"That you *know* about," Kirby corrected me with a smirk.

"I guess," I conceded. There was an awkward silence, and I decided this was the perfect moment to start stuffing popcorn into my face.

"So, which school do you go to?" asked Oliver, the brown-haired guy.

"It's . . . uh . . . Our Lady of the . . . Oaks," I said between chews and swallows. "Down in Grantville."

"Do you like it? It must be a big change from going to public school here with Jimmy," said Derek.

"Oh, it's complete torture," I assured him.

"Uh-huh. So you miss the boys, right? I *totally* get that," said Kirby, giggling. Oliver bopped him with a couch pillow.

"Well, no, not really," I said, finding myself unexpectedly puzzled. I leaned over and crushed Jimmy in a one-armed hug. "I mean, of *course* I miss this one, and I'm all for boys in general, but it's actually kinda nice not to have to worry about certain stuff. Like, it's so much *easier* with a uniform. You don't have to stand in front of your closet every morning hating your clothes. Plus, it's nice not having to worry about shaving your legs."

All four guys reared back in horror, and I couldn't help but laugh out loud.

"Gross, gross, gross," said Kirby, shuddering. "That's an argument for coeducation if I ever heard one." Then he leaned in conspiratorially. He may only be a 6.5, but he has totally amazing green eyes. "So, are there really no guys anywhere? Like, no cute volleyball coaches hitting on the horned-up girls or anything?"

"Well, my math teacher's a guy, but I don't think anyone would ever describe him as cute." I started picking at some popcorn between my front teeth. "Hmm, there are a few more guy teachers, but still, nobody who is in any way attractive. Otherwise . . . well, there's the play. We're doing *Into the Woods*. Auditions are next week, and it seems like everyone wants to be in it 'cause there'll be guys auditioning from other schools."

Jimmy tossed up a handful of popcorn so that it landed on Derek. "How 'bout you audition for Prince Charming?"

Kirby snorted, and Derek returned fire at Jimmy—my cue to seek cover on the floor. Pretty soon Kirby, Derek, and Jimmy were in a full battle, with Jimmy screaming, "It was a *compliment!*" Meanwhile, I was lying on the floor near Oliver, giggling.

"Prince Charming's not even a real role," I muttered to Oliver. He sent some popcorn their way, then held out a protective arm over me as the other three suddenly joined forces and started pelting us mercilessly.

We were laughing pretty hard, but when we finally caught our breath, Jimmy said, "No, seriously—why don't we all audition, too?"

Kirby pulled a sour face. "Uh, maybe because we have better things to do than schlep down to a Catholic girls' school in Grantville? They'll probably throw holy water on us to see if we melt." He turned to me to add, "No offense."

I threw up my hands and shrugged to show that no offense was taken.

But Jimmy had a look. I knew that look. It's somewhere between crazed and crazy. When Jimmy gets an idea, no matter how harebrained, he gets very attached to it. "Marty, that's a perfect way for us to spend more time together!"

"Jimmy, sweetie, didn't we try something similar in fifth grade?" I raised my eyebrows as high as they would go, hoping he would read my thoughts. And my thoughts at the moment were: THIS IS A TERRIBLE IDEA. DO NOT CONTINUE THIS LINE OF REASONING.

After a truly disastrous foray into theater in fifth grade

(an audition for *You're a Good Man, Charlie Brown*—trust me, you don't want to hear about it), Jimmy had stayed far away from any of the drama stuff I did. I mean, other than seeing me perform, of course. But at the moment it seemed he was ignoring both the past as well as my elevated eyebrows.

"Oh, fifth grade, schmifth grade," he replied, waving my objection away. "This is a genius idea! This way you'll have company, too!"

He turned to Derek. So, you know when hostages are forced to say stuff on camera, and it's super-obvious from their faces that they're being forced to say it? That was Derek's face at the moment.

"Sure! Sounds fun!" Derek finally said.

Oliver grinned. "Yeah, why not? Let's do it! I mean, it could be fun!"

Aww, these guys were so nice! I didn't know what to say. We all looked at Kirby.

"Well, you ladies do what you want," Kirby said, shaking his head. "But I'm not going to join your merry band in Nunville. No way, José."

The Tudor-style house was pretty impressive, with neatly trimmed topiary bushes lining the walkway up to the front door.

Ding-dong!

Click-click.

Creeeak.

"Hi, my name is Martha Sullivan. I, uh, go to school with Xiang. Um, I think she's expecting me?"

The gray-haired Chinese man just looked at me, completely expressionless.

Tick.

Tock.

Tick.

Tock.

Xiang suddenly materialized, squeezed past her father, grabbed my hand, and pulled me away from the front door and down to my dad's idling car. She looked amazing, with her hair down and wearing a sky-blue dress with a Peter Pan collar—I realized that I hadn't seen anyone from Oaks wearing anything except the school uniform or our gym clothes. I suddenly felt self-conscious about my boring red T-shirt and jeans. Why did I still dress like Dora the Explorer? I was almost fifteen, ferchrissake. That needed to change, and today was the perfect day to start.

"I'm so completely mortified. My dad is so weird," she murmured.

"I know exactly how you feel," I said, pointing to my waiting father—eyes closed, air-drumming the steering wheel to God-knows-which rock anthem. Xiang looked a little shocked.

I knocked on the windshield to bring Pops out of his reverie, then plopped myself into the passenger seat. Xiang slid into the back, extending her hand between me and my dad. He was busy doing some sort of head-banging thing, with no apparent sense of personal dignity or shame.

"Hello, Mr. Sullivan. My name is Xiang," she said in a bright, high voice, smiling a flight-attendant smile. She really laid it on thick for adults, apparently.

Dad tried to shake her hand, but he used his left hand and ended up grasping her fingers instead. Yeah: awkward. I started thinking maybe this was all a mistake. I mean, there was a definite risk that Xiang would never speak to me again after meeting my dorky dad. He finally released her hand and turned down the music (Queen's "Bohemian Rhapsody," as it turned out—no further comment necessary).

"Nice meeting you," he said. "It's great to see that our Marty is making friends at her new school." I glared at him, using my (unfortunately feeble) psychic powers to try to shut him up. God, could he be more lame? I wanted to send Xiang some sort of physical signal, to make it crystal clear that I was *not amused* by my dad, but she was busy rummaging in her purse.

She took out a tube of lipstick and started applying it as my dad peered at her through the rearview mirror. "Do your parents want you back by a certain time?"

Xiang made a pouty face. "Yeah, if I'm not back here by four, it's likely the planet will explode."

My dad smiled. "Rightee-oh. Then we'll shoot for three thirty to be safe. I mean, we have seven billion lives to think of—it's quite a responsibility!"

Groan.

Xiang moved on to applying mascara. "Um, thanks," she said.

Needless to say, I couldn't have been more relieved when the car finally pulled up to the mall entrance.

"Now, you girls be good. Marty, you got your cell?" I rolled my eyes and nodded. "Great. So I'll see you at this entrance at three o'clock sharp, 'K? Oh, and remember what I said about talking to—"

"Bye, Dad!" And with that, the door was closed, and I was pulling Xiang away from the car. The giant glass doors to the mall mercifully slid apart, allowing us to get *away* from that man. I let out a heaving sigh.

Xiang, weirdly, couldn't see how completely irritating my father was.

"Your dad is sooo nice," she said. I had no idea what she was talking about—her parents must torture her with yodeling or electric forks or . . . something.

Then she said, "And he is so cute!"

With those words, I spontaneously combusted into a mushroom cloud of fire all over the entrance of the mall, inflicting third-degree burns on a dozen nearby shoppers and melting several fake palm trees.

"*Excuse* me? You need help. Serious, long-term, psychiatric help."

Xiang tossed her hair and smiled, apparently demonstrating that she was quite happy, thank you, to be mentally ill.

Whatever.

We headed straight for the food court—we were starving, and since we only had three hours to power-shop, we definitely needed to load up on calories. We snagged a table by the fountain, with excellent people-watching potential. Xiang offered to hold the table while I got the food.

"Um . . . could you get me . . . a seven-layer burrito from Taco Bell? With a Coke. Oh, and a pintos-and-cheese, too. And four mild sauces. Oh, heck, get me a Meximelt, too. I'm hungry enough." Clearly, the girl wasn't afraid to eat. I loved it.

But when I finally made it back, I nearly died of shock. Our table was crowded . . . with six boys! Xiang was holding court over the group, and I had to squeeze myself past them to put the tray onto the table.

Xiang grinned at me. "Oh, Marty—great! Thanks," she said, but there was something weird about her voice; it was unnaturally babyish. "Let me introduce you to the guys!"

The *guys*? Like, her posse? Xiang is nothing if not full of surprises. First Jimmy and his "guys," and now Xiang—what was going on?

"This is Tim, that's Parker, Kevin, Chris, and Billy, and—ack, I forgot your name!"

A small, brown-haired fellow's face flushed. "George."

"George! Of course." Xiang turned to me. "He's in percussion, so we can't really even see each other at rehearsal."

Ohhhhhhhh. This was a Cleveland Youth Orchestra contingent. The world made sense again. They all looked like nice enough guys, but after a quick scan, I knew I wasn't looking at my future husband among them. They all kind of looked the same, with similar shaggy haircuts and slouchy jeans—no sparks here. Damn.

Oh, well, back to the business at hand. Boy musicians or not, I had a date with a Chicken Soft Taco.

"Do you play an instrument?"

I looked up, mid-bite, at . . . let's see, that would be . . . Chris? I shook my head, munching away.

Damn, that's a good taco.

"Marty's really into theater, though," Xiang interjected. Her new voice was starting to drive me nuts. "She's dragging me into joining the fall musical. We just haven't figured out how, since I can't do the onstage stuff, and I don't really want to do the backstage stuff."

Parker gave Xiang a quizzical look. "Well, why don't you just join the orchestra?"

Xiang and I bolted up in our seats as if someone had

Tasered us. Then I sprayed Chicken Soft Taco everywhere as we burst out laughing.

DUH! Why hadn't we thought of that before?

"Ohmigod, we are soooo dense," Xiang groaned.

"What's the show?" Parker asked.

"*Into the Woods*," I answered, slurping my Coke.

Xiang gasped. "I know! You guys should all try out, too! I don't know what kind of instruments they need, but I'm sure they need clarinets."

Pause. Everyone just looked at Xiang.

She turned bright red and rushed to add, "Oh, and drums and violins and stuff. Lots of different instruments. Not just . . . well, whatever. I'll find out which ones they need." By the time she finished speaking, Xiang had somehow managed to hide her entire body behind her small cup of pintos-and-cheese.

Parker, too, had turned a shade or two redder. "Yeah, that sounds good. Well, we should go," he said. "See you around." He abruptly stood and walked away. The other boys trailed after him.

"Uh, what was that?" I asked. "What did I miss?"

Xiang peered out from behind the refried beans, then slowly unfolded herself back into three dimensions.

"I just . . . ugh!" She buried her face in her hands. "I'm *such* a complete idiot."

Okaaaay . . . I guess that meant it was time for me to put down what was left of my Chicken Soft Taco. And I guess it was time for some Girl Talk, a skill I had never had the opportunity to master. Would a lifetime of watching romantic comedies be enough to go on?

"Xiang, what's wrong? What are you talking about?" I asked, tentatively rubbing her back.

"I just . . . well, it's Parker. I think I . . . well, I don't know. What do you think of him?"

"I, uh, I just met him," I replied uncertainly. "He seems nice, and he's cute, I guess." I wasn't sure what the correct answer was, but at least I got Xiang to nod, however sadly.

"So . . . I'm guessing he plays the clarinet?"

More sad nodding.

"And you like him?"

More sad nodding. (I'm awesome at Twenty Questions, by the way.)

"And this is a bad thing because . . . ?"

"My parents would totally, totally, totally freak out. He's not Chinese. They think I'm too young to even be thinking about boys, that I need to focus on school, and that American guys . . . oh, what am I even talking about? Parker and me? That's so far from happening, it's not even funny." She shook her head.

I rolled my eyes. Screw the sympathetic Girl Talk. "Xiang. Come on. Seriously. Get a grip. You wouldn't be the first teenager in the world to date someone her parents didn't approve of."

I nudged her.

"Right?"

Another nudge. "Am I right?"

Xiang took a deep breath. "You're right. You're right, you're right, you're right. But whatever. I don't even know if he likes me."

I gave her a hard stare in response.

"OK, maybe I can sort of tell that maybe he possibly likes me."

"Mmm. I thought so." I bumped up against her.

Xiang shoved back, harder. I found myself throwing my hands out defensively, laughing.

"OK, OK, OK, no fighting. Oh, look, Parker's coming back. Psych!"

Xiang shoved me again, and we finally settled down enough for me to finish my taco.

"Hurry up and eat," I told her. "We don't have that much time to shop."

An hour later, I still hadn't found anything that (a) looked cute, (b) fit, and (c) was even close to affordable. Seriously, it was like Maplewood Mall was conspiring against me, like it was some elaborate practical joke. Every time I saw a garment that seemed plausible as something I would *actually wear*, the store would be missing my size. Oh, but they would have it in another pattern—a totally hideous one.

Or, when the one I wanted actually did fit, the color would wash me out to the point of transparency. I swear, in some of those clothes, I could moonlight as an educational-science display, because you could totally trace my circulatory system.

Or, I'd have to sell my firstborn to be able to afford it. Seriously, were these skirts and dresses made of woven twenty-four-carat gold thread or something???

Basically, I needed a fairy godmother. Meanwhile, Xiang had no problem racking up armfuls of adorable, cheap clothes, often things that *I spotted first* but for whatever reason weren't right for me. On her, they were a perfect fit.

Bitch.

Seriously, though, hanging out with her was surprisingly easy. It turns out that I'm not missing the capable-of-being-friends-with-girls gene, and even though I had expected to be sad not shopping with Jimmy—like, would I be comparing Xiang to him the whole time?—it wasn't like that at all. Xiang was different. Not better, not worse, just different.

At one point, when we emerged from H&M, we stumbled over Xiang's oversize shopping bags . . . and directly into a little old lady. She gasped and staggered back as the two of us dropped the bags and steadied each other. Amazingly, we had narrowly escaped a full-on sprawl-fest on the floor.

"Sorry, so sorry!" said a deep male voice. I turned to see the source.

Tall? Check. Dark? Check. Handsome? Check *plus*.

"Sorry, she can't see very well," he said, gently grabbing ahold of the old lady by the arm and guiding her away. "Nanna, are you all right?"

"No, it was totally our fault—" I started to say, but he had already walked away with the woman, swallowed by the crowd.

Xiang wrinkled her nose in disgust. "Can you smell that? That lady was *rank*. She had totally pissed herself."

"Yeah, gross," I said. "But how cute was the guy?"

"He was?" Xiang rose up on tiptoe and craned her neck, trying to catch a glimpse of him. "I didn't notice."

I giggled. "You are *so* smitten, it's ridiculous. There is only one boy in your little world, and his name rhymes with . . ." Ah! Shoot, what does it rhyme with? ". . . blarker."

"You're such a dork," she said, shaking her head and smiling. "Blarker? Really? You could have said 'darker.' 'Starker.' Or 'marker'! Or even 'barker'; it's way better than *blarker*."

Boy, she was pretty good at rhyming on demand! She should be a rapper or something.

Wait a minute . . .

"You are so busted!" I said, pointing an accusing finger at her. "You've been writing *love poems* about him!" Ha!

Xiang flushed crimson. "What? I have no idea what you're talking about." She lifted up her bags and started hurrying away. "So, what stores haven't we done yet?"

*L*ater that day, after dropping Xiang off at her house (and barely surviving a dozen of Dad's "jokes" about avoiding Judgment Day), I was beat. Totally and completely drained.

Sadly enough, I had only managed to come away from our shopping run with two pairs of socks. True, they *were* cute—one pair had tiny grasshoppers right above the heel. No one would ever see them, probably, but *I* would know that my little Jiminy Crickets were with me. (OK, I *know* that was a fashion step in the exact wrong direction, but some habits die hard.)

But whatever! Even though I was a shopping failure, the trip was a social success. Xiang was cool. Unpredictable at times, and sometimes scary, but cool. When we gave up on finding any more clothes, she ducked into a bathroom to scrub her face back to normal, and I wasn't even that bothered when she smoked a cigarette as we waited for my dad. (I mean, I made her smoke behind a bush in case my dad showed up early, but still.)

Anyhoo . . . with Xiang back home with her parents, and me figuring that Mr. James Caradonna was out with his new Gay Friends, and my otherwise not having a life, I resigned myself to the fact that my Saturday night would be a sad smorgasbord of Lifetime movies and lame sketch-comedy shows.

Oh, well. I supposed life could be worse. I threw on my dad's old Walk for the Cure sweatshirt from 2010 and my pink-and-gray-plaid pajama bottoms and plopped myself down on the couch in the living room. I hid a contraband bag of Twizzlers under the blanket, and fifteen minutes into my attempt to figure out some Venezuelan soap opera on channel 661, the doorbell rang.

"Mo-omm! The door!" I yelled.

(What? Her office is closer to the door. Whatever.)

I heard her keyboard stop clattering, and shuffling footsteps, and the next thing I knew, somebody physically launched himself over the back of the couch and onto Yours Truly.

"My celestial spinach leaf!"

Oh, heavens. Jimmy.

"Stop it! You're breaking my ribs!" I screamed, laughing. He let loose with some tickling jabs.

Suddenly I heard, "Oh, I loooove *La Intrusa!*" Derek walked into the living room, with Oliver close behind. All three were decked out in snazzy shirts (Jimmy's literally sparkled), clearly prepared for some kind of event. Derek was carrying a big backpack and sporting what must be his "going out" hair (meaning, sculpted in gel into a messy spiky pattern that must've taken him fifteen minutes of fussing to achieve). Oliver wasn't wearing his cap this time, and I was really surprised to see how cute he actually was. He had wavy dark-chocolate-colored hair that girls would kill for and big puppy eyes that were just, I don't know, *friendly*.

Jimmy turned from the TV, asking, "So, you've learned a foreign language and you didn't tell me?"

Weirdly, I suddenly felt shy, having all these boys barge in to find me in my pj's snarfing candy on a Saturday evening.

"Oh, naw, I was just flipping through the channels . . . ," I offered lamely.

Derek shook his head. "No, no, this is great stuff. Watch out for Vittorio—he's a snake."

We all looked at him with giant question marks hanging above our heads.

"What? Telenovelas are great!"

Jimmy gave me another squeeze, murmuring, "How cute is he?" He grabbed a Twizzler and started gnawing on the end of it.

"Where's Kirby?" I asked. The night before, Kirby had totally stuck to his guns about not auditioning, despite all our best attempts to get him to change his mind.

"Oh, he's having boy troubles. He accidentally sent a message to his Omaha boyfriend that was *supposed* to go to his Cincinnati boyfriend," said Oliver, rolling his eyes.

Okaaay, I didn't know how to respond to that. Luckily, I didn't have to; Jimmy was giving me a once-over, and his disappointed facial expression said it all.

"You are soooo changing out of that . . . *arrangement* of fabric. Pronto."

"We're kidnapping you," said Oliver, extending a hand. "We're going out, and we're paintin' the town red!"

I gave him a doubtful look as I grabbed his hand and let him lift me from the couch. "Ah, I see. We're going to hop into your *car* and go drink *alcoholic* beverages all night? And how do you propose we do that, exactly?"

The boys just grinned in response.

"O ye of little faith . . . ," Jimmy muttered as he pushed me out of the room, toward my bedroom. "Now, let's see. Let's find you something low-cut and trashy . . ."

A couple of hours later I *was* painting the town red. One brushstroke at a time, that is, at Chippewa Elementary's playground. Oliver, it turned out, was a photographer for the Weeksburg High school paper, and they were planning a special section on the social lives of kids at the school— you know, sex surveys and articles about attitudes toward alcohol—that kind of thing. Since school policy didn't let the paper show actual alcohol or PDA, Oliver wanted to illustrate the section with photos of kids (i.e., us) taking expressions for "going out and partying" literally. He had prepared a big plywood sign with the words THE TOWN written with outlined letters, and he was taking flash pictures of me and Jimmy filling them in with red poster paint. He had already snapped pics of me walking onto a plank over the sign ("going out on the town"), several of Derek surrounded by overfilled garbage bags ("wasted"), and a few of himself about to be struck by a sledgehammer that I held over his head ("smashed"). There were still lots of props to go: a box of fishhooks (for "hooking up," of course), bottles of tomato paste ("getting sauced"), and a black T-shirt that simply read BLOTTO across the chest.

School policy did allow showing kids holding hands, though, so we had taken some shots of me leaning against Derek, our fingers intertwined. (Jimmy and I refused to hold hands. We loved each other deeply—but not like *that!*— and we were way too close to make a joke of it.)

Then Oliver insisted on taking some shots of Jimmy and Derek holding hands. "We *have* to include that," he said, grinning.

"But won't that look like Derek's a bit . . . all over the place?" I asked.

To have alternatives, we also took some photos of me holding hands with Oliver.

When Jimmy first insisted I wear something *revealing,* I was like, HELL no. I'm not going to be the only girl-skank in these pictures! But in the end, I figured it would look way worse if we did it halfway, and there's a lot to be said for being able to laugh at yourself. And, truthfully, we were having a total blast. I was wearing this absurd dress that I got for my Halloween costume last year—Glinda from *Wicked* (more widely known as the good witch from *The Wizard of Oz*). I hoped my strappy silver heels, big hoop earrings, and wide plastic bangles would mix it up enough to make it "a look." (Oh, and *of course* my legs were clean-shaven— hello!)

But as ridiculous as the outfit was, I did feel kinda hot. I mean, I'm pretty short, so I'll never be America's Next Top Model, but I'm also self-aware enough to know that I'm not *hideous*—I like to think of my face as vaguely elfin, with blue eyes, a slightly upturned nose, and a somewhat pointy chin. Maybe it was the poufy hair and makeup, maybe it was the Saturday-night vibe, or maybe it was the admiring stares I got from the boys after I emerged from the bathroom, but I just felt . . . free. And the mojo was *on* (albeit wasted on nice gay boys).

As I added the finishing touches to the *N* in *TOWN*, Oliver walked up behind me and asked, "Hey, Marty, wanna make out?" I turned to see that he was holding refrigerator magnets for the letters *U*, *T*, and *O* in one hand and a metal cookie sheet in the other.

"Anytime, babe," I replied, grinning.

Then we both realized that Derek and Jimmy really *were* making out, and that kind of sobered us a little.

"Break it up!" I called out to them. "We need a photographer here!"

Jimmy reluctantly detached himself from Derek's lips and made his way to the camera.

"So," I said to Oliver, jiggling the letter *T* on the tray, hoping it looked like we were arranging them.

"So," he replied.

"Do you have your own make-out buddy?" Even in the darkness, I could see Oliver's face turn crimson. I couldn't help but giggle—with the camera flashes and his big brown eyes, he really did look like a deer caught in headlights. "Other than me, that is."

"Well, I . . . um, I was just in a relationship, actually."

"Really? With someone at your school?"

He nodded.

"And good riddance, it's over. Charlie never treated you right!" Derek called out, then muttered, "Jerk."

Oliver looked a thousand more shades uncomfortable, and I could tell he was wishing for his baseball cap.

"Yeah . . . ," he said gamely, "I guess. Kirby says that, too."

"How long were you guys going out?" I asked.

"Two years."

Wow. That seemed like a long time, considering they must have started going out when they were—what? Twelve? Thirteen? That's pretty young for straights, let alone gays!

"How 'bout you? Are you seeing anyone?" he asked.

Jimmy snorted.

"Gee, thanks, Jimmy!" I said, tossing the *T* at him.

"Hey, you'd better watch it," he said, "or you'll be the one getting sauced, missy!"

"No, actually, it's about time we *all* got sauced . . . ," said Derek, opening up his backpack. He lifted out a six-pack of beer. ". . . thanks to my brother."

There wasn't enough alcohol there for us to get *actually drunk*, but I was soon buzzing happily. The stars were blazing above, the fireflies lazily echoed our camera flashes, and we were laughing uncontrollably, goofing around.

At some point, it occurred to me that this was a *mo-*

ment. Like, I needed to remember this night. Maybe it was the alcohol, but I started getting philosophical about it—I mean, you hear people say all the time that high school was "the best years of their lives." That always seemed super-depressing to me—I mean, is it really all downhill afterward?—but maybe there was some small kernel of truth to it. It's not like I ever saw my parents being this silly with their friends—did they miss being able to do this kind of stuff? Why *didn't* they ever get this silly anymore? Or did they?

My parents never really talked about their teenage years. Did other people's parents talk to them about their pasts? I doubted Xiang's ever did. Or Jimmy's parents. Maybe it was, like, my parents knew me so well that they thought I should be able to remember their pasts somehow, too, even though that was completely illogical. Huh.

But my parents didn't meet each other until after college, so did they even talk about it between themselves? Or maybe it was just an awkward thing to work into everyday conversations . . .

"Heads up!" A slice of bread sailed past my ear.

"Hey, hey, hey—watch it!" Oliver said, almost sternly, to Jimmy.

"What? I'm trying to get her 'toasted'!" Jimmy responded, grinning. "I know! Let's play Duck, Duck, Goose!" He looked around. "If only we had brought Grey Goose vodka. I think my parents have some in the liquor cabinet . . ."

"Sorry, beggars can't be choosers," Derek said, planting

a kiss on Jimmy's cheek. "And speaking of my brother, he said he'd be coming to pick us up around eleven thirty, so we should start packing up and head back. Who has the Listerine?"

The mention of Listerine made me think of the time I'd put mouthwash in Jimmy's Arizona iced tea bottle, and, unaware, he took a swig. He ended up spraying it all over his Ted Baker feather-design bedspread, which he had specially ordered online a few weeks before. He was *so mad*, I thought fuzzily, he didn't speak to me for a *whole day*. I never played a joke on him again.

"Yeah," said Oliver, watching me giggle moronically at my own thoughts, "I think we're all set with the photos. It's probably time to head back."

I told Xiang about the photo shoot during Monday morning's algebra class, and she was totally envious. Mr. Dartagnan was at the front of the room prattling on about integers, his glasses flashing in the projector's light and making him look like Dilbert. Meanwhile, everyone else in the room was in the midst of a REM cycle, just shy of actual snoring.

"God, why do *I* have to live in permanent lockdown?" Xiang grumbled. "After you guys dropped me off on Saturday, all I could do was watch some bad Spanish-language TV."

"*La Intrusa*?" I whispered back.

Xiang's eyes bugged out, à la Wile E. Coyote.

"Um, please tell me you're stalking me. I'm not sure I can be friends with someone who memorizes TV schedules."

"Miss Hsu?" At the sound of Mr. Dartagnan's voice, Xiang replayed the trick from Saturday of folding herself into a single point in space. "Anything you'd like to share with the rest of us?" He must have meant a royal "us," because no one else in the room bothered to wake up.

"No."

"Then will you and Miss Sullivan please stop your incessant chatter?"

He turned back to the projector. I made my most sympathetic "Oops!" face at Xiang, but she just shrugged and rolled her eyes.

We lay low for the rest of the class, but then later, at lunch, Xiang slid her tray in front of me, beaming. During her free period, she had gone to see Sister Mary Alice about being in the orchestra for the show.

"She. Is. So. Cool," Xiang gushed. "Have you seen her classroom? There are *couches* in there. And she has, like, snacks put out in bowls everywhere. I can't wait to take her English lit class next year." Xiang sat down and heaved her green messenger bag into the chair next to her. She had written *Albatross* across the front flap with a marker.

"But she said she doesn't even know how to play a kazoo, so she won't be the musical director. She's delegating all the music stuff to Mrs. Murray, the lady with helmet hair. And Sister Mary Alice actually said 'helmet hair' when she described her."

"*WHAT?* Really?" I snorted soy milk into my nasal cavities.

"No, of course not," Xiang said carelessly. "But I could tell she was *thinking* it. Apparently, they haven't set a date for auditions yet, but it'll probably be next week sometime. They weren't even thinking about opening it up beyond people who are already in the school orchestra, but I mentioned that I had friends from other schools who might be interested." She carefully lifted the plastic wrap off her sandwich.

"Ugh, that reminds me," I said, "the cast auditions are on *Wednesday*, and I have nooo idea what I'm going to do." I squished my face between the palms of my hands, and I could feel my heart speed up. I had spent all of yesterday afternoon at Bracksville Public Library's drama section, trying to find a good monologue. And what song would I sing? If I didn't get into this play, then . . . oh, God. I didn't even want to think about it. No Jimmy *and* no theater? Or worse, *Jimmy and the boys getting in and me not?* How embarrassing would that be?

Xiang looked up from her sandwich. "Don't look at me. All I have are, like, cello sonatas."

I frowned. "Any ideas for the monologue?"

Xiang shook her head. "I dunno. 'To be or not to be?' You know I don't have a clue about that stuff."

I pushed a raisin along the table with a piece of celery. "I just wish I knew what other people were bringing. I mean, if I come in with a monologue from something theater-y, like *Our Town* or *The Miracle Worker* or *The Effect of Gamma Rays on Man-in-the-Moon Marigolds* or something, will that make me super-lame?"

Xiang shot me a what-the-hell-are-you-even-talking-about look.

"Or is everyone going to be edgy and creative, doing dramatic readings from, like, a book on Demi Lovato's beauty tips?"

That made her smile. "That's really good! You should totally do that! I'm sure you'll stand out."

"Or be shunned as a freak forever."

"Or that," she conceded, and started sucking on her juice-box straw.

We sat in silence for a moment, imagining my potential social death.

"Oh, let's talk about something else," I finally said. A lightbulb went off in my head. "Heyyyyyy, didn't you have a CYO rehearsal on Sunday?" I twirled an accusatory carrot stick in her direction.

"Don't even go there," Xiang said, shaking her head.

"What? Did you even talk to him?"

"Yeah, I guess, a little bit," she hedged.

"Did you start the conversation, or did he?"

"Parker did."

I sat there, just looking at her. She looked right back at me, impenetrable.

"Aaaaand?"

"He came over during the break and said hey."

Another moment of just sitting. This was getting ridiculous.

"Xiang," I said, "you gotta work with me here. We'll be here until Saturday at this rate. Just tell me what happened."

Xiang rolled her eyes and gave a huffy sigh. "OK, OK, OK." Then she rattled off, "He came over, said hey, said it was great running into me and meeting you on Saturday, asked how long we ended up hanging out at the mall . . ."

"Well, that sounds promising!" I interjected.

". . . and he asked what I was doing on Wednesday after school."

Yowza!

"WHAT? Ohmigod, that's *huge!*" I exclaimed. But then I stopped myself. "Wait—are you lying again?" You could never tell with Xiang.

"Noooo, he really asked me that. But I told him that Wednesday I'm going to stay after school to watch your audition. And that was that."

"Oh, Xiaaaaaang . . ." I was touched, actually—she chose supporting me over a date with her crush! Gosh, would I have done that for her? Uh . . . no. "You know you didn't have to do that. I'll be fine auditioning on my own."

"Well, no shit, but I was glad I had an excuse. That sounded a lot better than, 'Actually, my mother expects me home right after school to practice this goddamn cello and do my fucking homework.'" I involuntarily scanned the cafeteria to make sure there were no teachers around to hear. But poor Xiang. I had never seen her so upset.

Then we just sat there for a bit—me searching for something to say, and Xiang twisting her straw to death. This may be weird, but to be honest, I felt jealous of her, just as I had with Jimmy. I didn't even have the excuse of being gay, or of having really controlling parents, and yet I was the only one without any romantic stuff going on. I know I wasn't interested in the orchestra guys, but how come none of them liked me? What was wrong with me? Wasn't

I pretty enough, or friendly enough? Was I destined to spend all my Saturday nights pretending to flirt with a bunch of gay guys?

"OK, well, what did Parker say after that?" I finally asked. "When you told him you would be at the audition?"

"He just kinda turned red and bolted. I don't know."

I made a frowny face and said, "Don't worry, we'll figure something out. And, hey, if he joins the musical's orchestra, think about all that extra time you'll have to flirt and canoodle during rehearsals!"

"Ha-ha," she replied sadly.

"Come on, Xiang, chin up! Keep a stiff upper lip!" I said, reaching across the table and giving her shoulder a light punch.

"What the hell does that even mean? Shouldn't it be a stiff *bottom* lip?" she asked, just as the period bell rang. I shrugged, and we gathered our garbage and headed out of the cafeteria, variously contorting our lips and tapping them to test their stiffness.

That evening Jimmy came over so we could do our homework together. Yeah, I know, we have different homework, but sometimes he needs to have people around when he does it—otherwise, he ends up watching HGTV or *Teletubbies* or something; he has very little self-discipline.

"You don't happen to know what caused the Whiskey Rebellion, do you?" he asked me, sprawled out over my bed with his American history work sheets.

"I dunno—something about taxes? Isn't all the early stuff about taxes?"

"Yeah, but there's something more to it. Federalism or something. I wish this thing had an index," he said, flipping through his textbook.

"Can't help you there. Ask me next year." (Our Lady has us take American history as sophomores.) I finished off the last exercise on my algebra problem set and plopped the pages onto a sprawling mound of papers. My desk was a mess, but what else was new? I woke my computer up and started scanning my playlists.

"I hate to interrupt your productivity streak, but I need you to listen to this," I said. "I'm thinking of singing this at the audition on Wednesday." I clicked on "Moonshine Lullaby" from *Annie Get Your Gun*. Bernadette Peters's voice floated into the room, rich and slow.

Jimmy closed his eyes and placed his history book over his chest.

I tried to imagine how the song would sound with just piano accompaniment and with my voice (which isn't terrible, but I'm no Bernadette).

As the final notes rolled to a stop, Jimmy murmured, "You put me in your bed, make me do homework, and then you play this song. Are you *trying* to put me to sleep?"

"Sit up!" I said, giving the bed a kick. Unfortunately, I only jostled the mattress a little.

"Oh, sure, now you're going to rock me?" Jimmy said, giggling.

"I'm serious—no sleeping! Are you saying the song is way too boring?"

"No, it's slow, but it's nice. It's perfect. Do you have sheet music for it?" Jimmy sat up and rubbed his eyes.

"Yeah, they had *Annie Get Your Gun* at the library—they have a surprising amount of musicals there. What are you auditioning with?" To be quite honest, I was still surprised that Jimmy planned to audition on Wednesday.

"Oh, I don't know. Is 'Happy Birthday' good enough?" he asked.

"Oh, come on. You'll never get a part if you don't even try," I said. I scrolled through my playlist. "How about . . . I know! 'More I Cannot Wish You' from *Guys and Dolls*! It sounds like 'Moonshine'—here." I clicked on it.

Jimmy gave me a doubtful look. "You want me to sound like I'm eighty years old?"

"Well, it'll be easier to put your own personal stamp on it, now, won't it?"

"Oh, don't worry. I'll stamp on whatever I end up singing."

"Ha-ha." I scrolled down the list of songs again. "Hmm . . . how about . . . *this* one?" I clicked on "Putting It Together" from *Sunday in the Park with George*.

Jimmy rolled his eyes as the song began. "Waaaay too complicated."

"Well, it's Sondheim, just like *Into the Woods*."

He didn't respond, just flipped absently through the pages of his history book.

"So you had a good time on Saturday, right?" he asked.

I kept scrolling through my list. "Yeah, of course! Didn't you?" This one was too high for Jimmy's voice. This one, too fast. Too operatic. Too girly . . .

"Yeah. Derek's brother is good people. What do you think of Oliver?"

"Oliver? He's nice! And super-cute, to boot." I looked up at Jimmy. "You know, I like Derek's friends, if that's what you're getting at."

Jimmy smiled dreamily. "Yeah, he does have good friends, doesn't he?"

"So what's with Kirby and the two boyfriends?"

"Five."

"What? *Five* boyfriends?"

"He hasn't met any of them, though. They're all long-distance, online relationships. But he's working the odds, assuming that most of them are catfishing or having lots of other relationships, too."

"I guess it's pretty hard to meet gay guys our age around here, huh?"

"Lucky me!" Jimmy said, grinning so wide it looked painful.

"Yeah, yeah, lucky you," I grumbled. "Ooooh, how about this?" I clicked on Ella Fitzgerald's version of "Bewitched, Bothered, and Bewildered." "I don't know what show it's from, but I'm sure you could find the sheet music for it."

But eight seconds into it, I clicked it off. "OK, maybe not."

Not that Jimmy heard it; he was busy doodling a heart

motif on his history notebook, lost in his thoughts. Geez Louise, why was everyone around me so lovesick all of a sudden? What about *me*? Whom did *I* have to swoon over?

I pulled a Twix bar out of my bottom desk drawer—I'd been saving it for a self-pity party just like the one I felt coming on. Then I double-clicked on Streisand's "What Kind of Fool," because I knew that Jimmy hated it.

*B*ut I didn't have to pity myself for long. No, sir, I was about to swoon, too.

Hard.

On Wednesday, I was buzzing with nerves all throughout the day, thinking about the auditions. Needless to say, I really, really, really, really wanted to be in the musical. Acting is the one thing that I'm actually good at. Not sports, not grades, not being all sexy and boyfriend-y. Nobody really paid much attention to me at school, but if I could just show everyone that side of me, it would change everything. I'd be Marty, that girl who was really great in the musical. (OK, I know that probably doesn't sound so great to most people, but at least it's something.)

But if I didn't even get into the musical, I'd just be . . . yeah.

I would *not* be able to stomach sitting in the audience, watching other girls perform onstage, let alone any of my gay boys. Even if no one else noticed or cared, I'd be humiliated for myself. I mean, when I was eleven, I staged a full reenactment of *Chicago* with dolls and stuffed animals—yes, disturbing in retrospect—for Jimmy and my parents. Last year, I used my birthday money to buy a Carol Channing–autographed theater program on eBay. I know all the words to basically every musical worth seeing, and a lot of the bad ones, too. I *had* to get a part.

So when I met Xiang at her locker after the last class, I was practically levitating with stress. I thought I was hiding it pretty well, but she looked at me uncertainly.

"Are you gonna be OK?"

"Yeah, no problem. I'll be fine." It was a bit mortifying to have Xiang see me like this, but there was only so much I could do about it. I took a deep breath, but it only made me feel even more light-headed. We floated out to the parking lot, where we saw Jimmy, Derek, Oliver, and Kirby standing around, looking lost.

"Oh, good, you got here in good time!" I shouted as we approached.

But I didn't stop. I just glided on past the boys toward Jerry Hall, and the boys grabbed their bags and hustled after us.

When we walked into the theater, I was relieved to see that there weren't as many girls there as at the meeting the week before—not yet, at least. I mean, don't get me wrong, there were still a lot of them, probably thirty or so. Maybe the process of finding a song and a monologue had weeded some of them out? There were only about a dozen boys so far, and clumps of them huddled in various corners.

Actually, it was weird to see boys in Jerry Hall—or anywhere at Our Lady, for that matter. I had gotten used to the girls' club feel of the place, and now it seemed like they were invading our space.

Jenny McCafferty was sitting on the edge of the stage, hollering, "Ladies, sign up here! Gentlemen, your sign-up sheet is on stage right! That's over there, for you theater newbies." She waved her arm broadly, as if she were directing 747s on a tarmac. "Have your sheet music ready, if you have it! And please, please, *please* make sure the pages are in order! I'm saying that for your benefit, of course." She did some sort of a pantomime of shuffling papers wildly and then gave a fake-sounding laugh. Xiang and I looked at each other, pitying. It was so bad, it wasn't even worth mocking.

But Jenny didn't seem perturbed by the awkward silence, and she plowed on. "OK, here's how this works. I'll be sitting over there by the entrance with the sign-up sheet, so late stragglers won't interrupt the process. When I call out your name, go to the piano and give Christy your sheet music. If you have sheet music, that is."

She motioned toward a pale girl sitting at the piano.

"Then go up onstage, introduce yourself, and work your magic." And she actually did a jazz-hands motion. "If you don't have a monologue prepared, as you should, there are a few emergency monologues you can read that I've put in a pile right here. Callback lists will be e-mailed out tonight or tomorrow morning, and callback auditions will take place on Monday—same time, same place."

I signed my name and e-mail address on the list, and our group settled in a far corner of the theater, near where Xiang and I had sat before. But I couldn't actually sit down in my buzz-y condition; I just sort of hovered above the group. I noted that Sister Mary Alice and Mrs. Murray, the musical director, had set themselves up in the second row, smack in the center, with their clipboards at the ready.

Kirby held out his hand to Xiang. "Hi, I'm Kirby."

"Oh, right!" I gasped. "I totally forgot. I'm sorry. Boys, this is Xiang. Xiang, this is Kirby, Oliver, Derek, and Jimmy."

Xiang wiggled her hand in a quick wave, then said to Kirby in her high, babyish voice (not again!), "I didn't see you sign up with the others. Aren't you auditioning, too?"

At that moment, I literally smacked my forehead with the palm of my hand. I turned to Kirby. "Ohmigod, you're actually here! I didn't even think about it—you're totally auditioning! We convinced you!" (To be fair, I wasn't noticing much of anything, as I was focusing on trying to respond to the earth's gravitational pull.)

Kirby smiled and shook his head. "Naw, I'm just here to provide immoral support."

"Boooooooo," I countered with an exaggerated frown and a double thumbs-down. "It's not too late!"

"Oh, leave him alone. That's exactly why I'm here, too," squeaked Xiang. "So, are you all freshmen?"

"Jimmy and Derek are," Oliver replied, "but Kirby and me are both sophomores. Kirby drove us here, actually."

For a moment, I felt the buzz dim a bit. They were *sophomores*? Kirby could *drive*? I had simply assumed that they were our age. Huh.

More people streamed into the theater, and I was back to vibrating—with a vengeance. I hated being this nervous. Each time someone walked in, my inner self kicked an inner wall. *Crap. More competition.* The separate groups in the audience were starting to coagulate into one big crowd.

And then *he* walked in.

My mental kick froze, and I registered his appearance: OH. MY. GOD.

My right arm flailed out instinctively, hitting Xiang.

"Ow!" she yelped, recoiling from my blow.

"That's the guy!" I hissed. *"That's the guy from the mall!"*

"What guy?" she asked, rubbing her left arm and glaring at me.

"You know! *The guy with the stinky grandmother!"*

She turned and peered thoughtfully at him but then shrugged. "If you say so."

Mall Guy made a brief scan of the crowd, then bent over Jenny McCafferty's list. For once, McCafferty seemed a bit subdued as she watched him sign his name. I thought I could sense a slight hush over the theater as he walked from the sign-up sheet to the other side of the stage, and it seemed as though heads throughout the audience tracked him like flowers following the sun.

Then I heard Kirby whistle softly behind me; he, too, was gawking at the guy. But who could blame him? Mall Guy had a lanky, tall build and shiny black hair that swept past eyes that were dark and soulful, even from fifty feet away. Jimmy grabbed my hand and squeezed it, raising his

eyebrows toward the newcomer. I responded by fanning my
face with my other hand.

Mall Guy had come in with a friend, a barrel-chested guy
with painfully spiked hair who chewed gum in an exaggerated, rolling motion. They settled on seats just at the edge of
the stage, along the aisle.

I turned and saw Oliver reach out and wipe Kirby's chin
with his hand.

"Looks like you've got some drool there, buddy."

After a few more people meandered in, Jenny stood and
let out a piercing whistle.

"OK, people! Shush! We're gonna get started now!" I
somehow managed to lower myself into my seat. Jenny
made a big show of checking the sign-up sheet. "The first
person to go is . . . Maria Kilkenny."

A big girl wearing bright orange socks hurried over to
the piano. She gave Christy her music and climbed up onto
the stage. I breathed a sigh of relief that they were going in
order—how many names were ahead of mine? Thirty-five
or so? God, that seemed like a long time—sitting and waiting, feeling like this . . .

"Hi, um, I'm Maria Kilkenny. I'm a freshman here, and
I'm going to sing 'There's a Fine, Fine Line' from the mu-
sical *Avenue Q.*" Ooh, excellent choice, I thought to myself.
And then she opened her mouth—and I almost died.

She was amazing. She was, like, *professional* amazing.

I got chills listening to her. Then her monologue, something from *Sophie's Choice*, was friggin' perfect. I mean, one

minute we were watching a stocky Oaks girl in orange socks, and the next thing we knew, Meryl Streep was standing on our stage, remembering the Holocaust.

Then I just felt sick. Was everyone going to be this good? Suddenly this whole audition thing seemed like a really dumb idea.

But that sinking feeling was buoyed by the next person to audition, a little guy wearing a St. Augustine's Prep letter jacket. He basically croaked his way through "Music of the Night" . . . or at least I think that's what it was supposed to be. And his monologue, taken from one of the court scenes from *A Few Good Men*—well, let's just say it wasn't *convincing*. Halfway through, Xiang put on earphones and took her algebra problem set out of her green bag.

Fortunately for those of us still watching through our fingers, none of the following people were that bad. Also fortunately, they weren't nearly as good as that Maria Kilkenny girl. There were some funny monologues and some pretty decent singers, and the choices weren't bad—well, except for a Disney song or two. A few people missed cues and forgot lines, but I was impressed (or *de*pressed, I should say) by how good everyone was.

There was this one senior, Kate O'Day, who really stood out. Tall, skinny, and blessed with long, straight auburn hair, she could have been a supermodel, and she carried herself like one. She sang "Popular" from *Wicked*, a song she was perfect for, since it's all about being pretty and, well, popular. Her monologue was from the montage at the end of the movie *Clueless*, when Alicia Silverstone realizes that she loves her stepbrother. Side note: No matter how much I love that movie (with all my heart and soul), or how cute Paul Rudd is in it (very extremely), the quasi-incest still creeps me out.

Kate did a good job, but I could tell she was angling for the Cinderella role, and I found that annoying. Anyway, her clique of friends cheered her in an obnoxious way—not so much to praise her performance but to intimidate everyone else.

And then, eventually, Jenny called my name.

My stomach did some gold-medal gymnastics as I clumped down the steps to the stage. I got up there but then realized I was still holding the sheet music. (Note to self: Follow self-evident instructions.) I heard Jenny heave an exaggerated sigh, and I didn't have to look at her to know she was rolling her eyes. Christy smiled sympathetically as I hustled to get her the music, and I tried to pretend that I still had a scrap of dignity as I remounted the stage.

Big breath, big breath.

"Hi, I'm Marty—Martha—Sullivan. Uh, I'm a freshman here. And I'm going to sing 'I Can Hear the Bells' from the musical *Hairspray*." Sister Mary Alice watched me impassively. I cleared my throat, and Christy started to play. (A little slow for my taste, but, hey, what could I do?)

It went OK, I guess. Could have been worse.

When I finished, Mrs. Murray scratched furiously at her clipboard with her pen, her lips pursed. Sister Mary Alice kept her eyes on me, her face a complete blank. Then I realized that Xiang and the boys were clapping and cheering at the back of the theater, and a hiccup of a smile made its way through me. Then my eyes wandered over to my left, where I saw Mall Guy looking at me with a lopsided grin. He had his arms raised in the air, clapping. I held his gaze, and my smile blossomed into full-on beaming.

Then it was time for my monologue, which also went fine. I ended up choosing Clarence Darrow's final argument in *Inherit the Wind*, which I figured was both theater-y and unconventional, since I was crossing gender lines. When I finished, I raised my head and gave a quick smile. My corner of friends broke out in cheers again, and I scuttled off the stage, but not without a sidelong glance (or two) toward Mall Guy. He was just so . . . magnetic.

Next up was Jimmy, and as my nervousness trickled down into calm, he slowly made his way to the stage. I hollered a solid "Whoo!" of support from my seat, but I could tell he was bracing himself for disaster.

"My name is James Caradonna. I'm a freshman at Bracksville High." Jimmy cleared his throat, and Christy started playing.

And his audition was terrible. I wish it hadn't been, but it was. *Really* terrible.

Red-faced, he climbed back up to where we were sitting, and I could tell that no amount of our clapping could take away the humiliation. Then I noticed Derek slip Jimmy a cough drop. Jimmy's hand lingered on Derek's fingers.

Then the next name was called out, and Derek reluctantly broke away to make his way down the auditorium steps to the stage.

"Hi, I'm Derek Mylvaganam, and I'm, uh, a freshman at Weeksburg High." Derek shifted from foot to foot as Christy pounded out the intro. Clearly, he was in the lowest level of hell. My whole body was clenched in sympathy as he began singing.

Wow. He was . . . not bad! Not bad at all. I mean, he looked like he'd rather be cleaning toilets at a Greyhound bus station, but his singing was totally great. Even Jimmy was surprised—his mouth was literally open, his slack jaw dangling.

When he finished, we whooped and hollered as we had for Jimmy. But Derek couldn't even look up at us, he was so mortified.

"Uh, and I'll be reading a monologue from A Raisin in the Sun."

Except that he looked more like he was removing his own skin with a guitar pick instead. The boy seriously did not want to be on that stage.

Jimmy reached over and grabbed my hand, giving it a death squeeze until Derek finally stopped. He had barely finished speaking the last word before he zoomed off the stage and back to his seat.

Kirby grabbed Derek's shoulders from behind and shook him while the rest of us bombarded him with oh-my-god-you're-so-good!s. We didn't even hear Jenny McCafferty call out Oliver's name the first time.

"IS THERE AN OLIVER KAPLAN HERE?" she repeated, waving her sign-up sheet at the audience.

Oliver leapt up from his seat and jogged down to the stage, but not before Kirby had flicked off Oliver's baseball cap.

"I'm here! I'm here! Sorry about that . . ."

He slapped his music in front of Christy and vaulted onto the stage. He flashed his bright white smile at Sister Mary Alice and Mrs. Murray.

"Hey, there. I'm Oliver Kaplan, I go to Weeksburg High, just like Derek up there. He was good, wasn't he?"

"Your song, Mr. Kaplan?" asked Sister Mary Alice. I couldn't see her expression, but I'd bet it wasn't amusement.

"Right—my song. I will be singing 'Slow Boat to China.'" He made a big show of clearing his throat, then swung a pointed finger at Christy. "Christy, take it away!" He gave her a big wink.

Oh, Oliver. What a card.

Christy giggled and started bouncing out the intro.

Oliver's grin didn't leave his face for a second. His pitch, on the other hand, was all over the place. The boy was apparently tone-deaf.

But that didn't slow him down at all: He did a cute little swaying thing, with his palms out, as if he were some sort of 1940s showman. Actually, he looked like he was having a ball, completely ignoring his own inability to produce an actual melody, and the joy was infectious. Even Xiang was watching him with a big, silly grin.

When Oliver finished, he gave a grand, sweeping bow, and it wasn't just our group giving him a rousing cheer. He put one hand over his heart and pointed at Christy with the other. "Christy, ladies and gentlemen! Let's hear it for Christy!"

Who knew he was such a ham?

Unfortunately, Oliver's acting skills weren't much of an improvement over his voice. He talked his way through his monologue in a stilted way, completely overemphasizing random words and rushing through the wrong parts. But he took another deep bow afterward, beaming his adorable smile and blowing kisses to the audience.

When he got back up to our group, he snatched his baseball cap back from Kirby and sank into the seat next to me.

"Whaddyathink?" he asked me, grinning.

I chuckled and gave him a sidelong glance. "You're full of surprises—I'll give you that."

Derek leaned over and whispered at the group, "OK, all of us have auditioned. Can we leave now?"

Jimmy looked at me, and I involuntarily looked over toward where Mall Guy was sitting.

"Uh, yeah, you guys can go," I said. "I'm gonna stick around and see the rest of the auditions—my dad's coming at eight to pick me up, anyway. Plus, we can't all fit in Kirby's car, right?" I turned to Xiang. "But you could go with them."

Xiang looked at me like I was nuts. "Uh, thanks but no thanks. I'm staying as long as possible. I'm in no rush to get home."

Oliver and Jimmy looked torn about whether to stay, but Derek was already standing and slinging his bag over his shoulder. Jimmy gave my hand a final squeeze as he trailed after Derek.

Oliver turned to me and said hurriedly, "You did really, really great. I was really impressed. See ya!" Then he followed Kirby down the steps. I noticed that Kirby was looking over to where Mall Guy was sitting, trying to get one final look at the beautiful boy.

Xiang scooched over to sit next to me. "Your friends are really nice. And they're so cute! Especially Oliver."

"Yeah," I agreed, smiling. "It's too bad he plays for the other team."

"Well, it looks like you've got your eye on another player altogether," she said accusingly, angling her head toward Mall Guy.

"What? Him?" I sputtered, totally unconvincingly.

"Uh-huh," she teased. "You're not as subtle as you think you are."

Well, I'm not the only one, I thought, scanning all the girls in the audience who had been sneaking glances at him throughout the evening.

There weren't that many people left to audition, and soon they called up Matt Berzinski, who turned out to be the big guy who had come in with Mall Guy. He was a mess—the song was barely comprehensible, and he read from one of the extra monologue sheets in exactly one tone of voice the whole time.

Then Jenny called out, "Felix Peroni." The tall, dark, handsome stranger from Maplewood Mall sauntered up to the stage.

"Hi, I'm Felix," he said to Sister Mary Alice, his voice as deep as I remembered. "I'm a junior at St. Paul's with Matt. This evening I'm going to sing 'Some Enchanted Evening' for you. Christy . . . if you please?"

Xiang huffed, "Didn't we already see Oliver do that whole 'banter' thing?"

I shushed her.

This guy wasn't just hot; he was good. His singing was amazing. And he knew it. And the girls in the audience knew it. The supermodel girl, Kate O'Day, stood and gave a piercing whistle during the applause.

His monologue was from some play I'd never heard of, and he breezed through it. He turned his dark eyes on Sister Mary Alice and gave her a news-anchor grin. "Thank you very much. I look forward to hearing from you."

This guy was confident—that was for sure.

As he made his way back to his seat, he looked over the audience, and for a moment his eyes met mine. And I couldn't tell if it was my imagination or not, but I thought I saw the shadow of a wink. Like, his cheek went up for a split second to create the slight *suggestion* of a wink.

That, or he had a twitch.

But I wanted to believe it was a wink.

Date: Thursday, September 10

To: undisclosed recipients

Subject: INTO THE WOODS CALLBACK LIST

Hi, Jenny McCafferty here, with the results of our first audition (attached).

Thanks so much to everyone for coming—it was a huge success! Woo-hoo!

Unfortunately, there are only eighteen roles in the musical, so we can't have everyone take part onstage. But if you don't find your name on the callback list, or if you don't make it to the final cast after the callback audition, there are other ways to be part of the OLOTO fall musical: **There are two assistant stage manager positions still open,** as well as positions in set design, props, costumes, orchestra, and so on.

If your name IS listed, callbacks will be held on Monday, September 14, at Jerry Hall, 3:45 P.M. SHARP.

Keep on keepin' on,

Jenny

P.S. Go, Acorns!

I took a deep breath before I opened the attachment. My mental drumroll was still rumbling in my head when I saw it halfway down the list:

Martha Sullivan.

Woo-hoo, indeed! Fun! Fun! Fun!

Let's see, let's see: Gosh, Kate O'Day . . . Maria Kilkenny . . . Derek Mylvaganam! Ah, there he was: Felix Peroni. (Oh, of course he was there!)

Hmm, there was no James Caradonna. No Oliver Kaplan, either.

Crap. Crappity-crap-crap.

(But yay for me!)

On Friday night, Xiang told her parents she was coming over to my house to work on a school project. If by "school project" she meant going over to Jimmy's house to watch Bollywood movies with me, Derek, Oliver, and Kirby, then, no, it wasn't a lie. Xiang spent about fifteen minutes changing her clothes and putting on makeup at my house before we left for la Casa di Caradonna. I realized that with all her practiced primping, this girl could be a very good influence on me.

But then, as we were walking through the woods to Jimmy's, Xiang pulled a cigarette out of her purse and smoked it. So maybe not.

Jimmy's sister, Jeanie, answered the door. This time she was decked out in riding boots and an equestrian helmet, and she flicked a riding crop against her leg impatiently.

"They're in the drawing room," she said archly, putting on a thick British accent so *drawing* ended up with a few more syllables than you would think.

"Er, you mean the den?"

Jeanie simply sniffed and stalked away. Xiang asked me where she rode horses around here.

"Oh, probably nowhere. Jeanie's just . . . odd."

Kirby and Oliver hadn't come yet, but Derek was very much there. He and Jimmy were sucking face on the couch when Xiang and I walked in.

"Break it up, break it up!" I said, shoving Jimmy aside so I could sit between them.

What? Oh, whatever, they see each other all the time.

Xiang sat down on a big cushion on the floor. "Hey, Derek, congratulations on getting the callback!" she said.

Derek didn't look particularly thrilled about it, but he mumbled his thanks. I squeezed Jimmy with one arm, saying, "Aww, and a big thank-you to you, Mr. Caradonna, for auditioning. I know it wasn't easy . . . for any of us."

Jimmy stuck his tongue out at me. "Ha-ha. Well, what're you gonna do? It was worth a shot."

"I'm surprised Oliver didn't get called back. I mean, he definitely connected with the audience," I said.

Jimmy seized my arm suddenly. "Hey, do you know if that super-attractive guy got called back?" he asked.

Derek jabbed him in the side.

"Ow," said Jimmy, laughing, "I mean, *supposedly* super-attractive guy."

"Who?" I asked as innocently as I could. There was a collective groan. I clearly wasn't fooling anyone.

"You know who. Mr. Dreamboat!"

"Oh, she knows all right," Xiang said. "His name's Felix, and yes, he was called back."

Damn her. Traitor.

"Is he gay?" I blurted out.

Derek and Jimmy looked at me blankly.

"You're asking us?"

"Yeah, ya know, aren't you supposed to have gaydar or something? Oh, don't you give me that patronizing look. I think that's a legitimate question."

Jimmy just chuckled, shaking his head.

"We'll have to defer to the expert," said Derek. "Oh, and—speak of the devil—I think I hear him now."

Just then, Kirby walked in, trailed by Oliver.

Kirby was wearing Oliver's baseball cap backward, with his red hair poking out in front. It looked so . . . ridiculous.

"What's up, mah bitches?" he barked at us, swaggering into the room.

Xiang gave Kirby a withering look that surprised even him. He broke character, erupting into a peal of laughter. "I'm so kidding. I'm—I don't—hey, good to see you again." He removed Oliver's hat, covering his face to hide it from where Xiang sat. "She's scary," he hissed at me, grinning.

"And don't you forget it," I replied.

"Hey, Kirby," Derek said, "Marty wants to know if that guy you were ogling at the audition yesterday is gay."

"It's a *legitimate question!*" I cried out, giving Derek a bop with a couch pillow.

"Of course he is. Everyone's gay," Kirby replied without hesitation.

Um, OK?

"Oh, don't listen to him," Oliver interjected. "His grand theory on life doesn't really make sense."

"It's just a question of time. And opportunity," Kirby continued. "And I, for one, would like an opportunity with that guy."

"And he's not the only one," Oliver said, shaking his head, laughing.

"Why? Who's after my man?" Kirby asked in mock alarm.

"No, I meant that that guy's not the only one you want an opportunity with."

Kirby rolled his eyes and jiggled his head a bit. "Well, *duh.* I'm *breathing.* But that guy was something, huh? He get called back?"

"Yup," Xiang said. "Oh, and, Oliver, you were totally robbed. You should have been called back."

Oliver held his hands out, palms up. "Well, what are ya gonna do?"

"That's exactly what I said!" Jimmy exclaimed. Then he turned to Xiang. "But what about me? I was robbed, too!"

I patted him on the head. "Yes. Yes, you were. Robbed."

He pushed me away, giggling.

* * * * *

The movie, I'm sure, was top-notch Bollywood fare, but I don't remember anything about it. Kirby kept yelling things at the characters on-screen, and soon we were laughing so hard we kind of lost track of the plot. If there even was one. It started off being about some girl liking some guy but her parents disapproving, of course, because they had picked someone out for her already. But then there were all these bizarro dance sequences, and even the characters seemed to stop caring about the story. So it wasn't long before we were up on our feet and imitating their dancing. (Xiang, by the way, can really bust a move. I don't know where she picks these things up!)

Jimmy had bought some samosas on his way home from school, and everyone except the lovebirds abandoned the movie halfway through for the kitchen.

"So. Xiang." Kirby launched himself next to where Xiang was sitting on the counter. She gave him a sidelong glance, chewing her samosa. "How is *your* whole drama going?"

Xiang's eyes flew to me, accusing. "You told them!"

My jaw dropped. "I did not!"

Kirby chuckled. "Aha! There *is* something!" He nudged her with his elbow. "Oldest trick in the book. Go on, tell Uncle Kirby."

"You don't have to tell him anything. Kirby, leave her alone," said the refrigerator. Actually, it was Oliver—he was trying to extract a Diet Coke from somewhere in the very back.

"Oh, come on. It's *Friday night*. I need some entertainment here!" Kirby turned back to Xiang and put his hand on her knee. "So I'm going to take a big leap and say it's about a man."

Xiang looked at him uncertainly but then nodded.

[Insert expectant silence here.]

Oh, Lord. I wasn't about to sit through Twenty Questions all over again.

Hand on hip, I huffed, "OK, fine, if you're going to tell him, I'll save us all a lot of time and give the condensed version. Parker Something-or-other, brown hair, slim, normal height . . . bluish eyes? Plays the clarinet in Cleveland Youth Orchestra with Xiang. And he's been asking if she's available for extra-orchestra activities."

I stuck my tongue out at Xiang in response to her glare.

"I'll bet!" Kirby said, grinning. "And what *exactly* is keeping these extra-orchestra activities from happening?"

"Kirby, lay off. Don't be so nosy. Some people like to let things . . . *develop*," Oliver said, cracking open the Diet Coke.

Kirby rolled his eyes. "Let me know how that works out for you," he muttered.

"Actually, my parents are anti-love—of any kind. Until I'm about thirty years old," Xiang said glumly.

Kirby snorted in exasperation. "Seriously? Geez, if my parents knew of my, er, *Greek proclivities*, they'd crucify me." He raised a campy eyebrow. "And I can assure you, that hasn't been a deterrent in the least. Five boyfriends and counting."

"You have five boyfriends?" Xiang asked, incredulous.

"Well, in theory," Oliver said. "He hasn't met any of them in person yet."

"I suppose that does make it easier," Kirby allowed. He turned to Oliver. "But you shut up. If my parents were like yours, I wouldn't have any problems!"

Oliver snorted, almost sneezing Diet Coke. "Oh, don't even—you would *so* not get away with having multiple boy-friends."

Kirby rolled his eyes and shrugged. "Still. You know what I'm saying."

I wish I could tell you what Xiang had to say about Kirby's virtual harem, but I was already halfway down the hall on my way to the bathroom, bursting. And when I got back, they had moved on to some ice cream they'd found, chatting away about the relative merits of Dunkin' Donuts versus Krispy Kreme. But Xiang seemed to have a new twinkle in her eye, so it seemed that Kirby might have been just what the doctor ordered as far as advisers go . . .

y the time callbacks rolled around on Monday, I was soooo ready for them to be over and done with. There are only a certain number of times you can try to match the list of callback people with the cast list in your head before you make yourself truly bonkers.

For better or worse, I ended up spending much of the weekend at the library, trying to find stuff on nutrition history for my global studies course. But I won't bore you with the details (they actually involve microfiche files), so let's just skip ahead to Monday afternoon.

So the final bell rang, and I raced over to my locker to shove some of the afternoon books in and take out even more books from the morning for homework. (Grrrrrr.) I shot into the bathroom for a bit of hair-fluffing in front of the mirror and then raced across the parking lot to Jerry Hall. This time it would be just me on my own, with no Xiang or Jimmy for support.

(Well, there would be Derek. Not that Nervous Nelly would be helping matters for me.)

I was almost at the door when I saw Felix (hubba-hubba) getting out of a silver Toyota. There was a pretty brunette in the front seat wearing a burgundy V-neck sweater that

I recognized as being part of the Holy Name uniform. (I can't believe I knew these things after only a few weeks at a Catholic school. Shoot me, please?)

My heart sank. Did he have a girlfriend?

Felix gave a halfhearted wave to the girl and walked into Jerry Hall ahead of me. Once I was inside, I saw that he was still in the lobby area, riffling through the books in his bag. He looked up at me and flashed me a dimpled smile that was blinding even as my eyes were still adjusting to the indoor light level.

"You don't have a pen I can borrow, do you?"

"Oh, um, sure!" I flushed, but I managed to sling my bag down my arm to crash onto the floor.

"I meant to grab one from my sister's car, but I forgot," he continued, and my heart took flight once again. *His sister!*

Stooping down, I rummaged for a pen, which I handed to him. He hesitated, and I realized to my horror that I was giving him a pen that had been horribly mutilated by my teeth—like, it was dented everywhere, and the little clip-y part on the cap was twisted at a strange angle and jagged with dentally inflicted wounds.

I know, I know, it's a gross habit, but I can't help it! I could just imagine how grossed out he was. All it needed was a layer of saliva on it, and it could have been a dog's chew toy.

I quickly pulled it back and lamely said, "Oh, that one doesn't work . . . um . . . there's another one in here some-where . . ." Finally I managed to pull out a reasonably un-molested pen and gave it to him.

"Thanks. And I'm Felix." His low voice was mesmerizing.

"Marty. I mean, Martha. Hi." I followed him into the auditorium, hating myself.

Inside, Jenny McCafferty was onstage, discussing something with Sister Mary Alice and Mrs. Murray. There were already two dozen or so people sitting in the seats.

"Guess we're right on time, huh?" Felix said aloud.

Was he talking to me? Oh, my gosh, he was.

"Oh, yeah," I said. You can see why I'm known for my sparkling wit.

He dropped into a nearby seat, looked up at me, and patted the seat next to him. I was still thrown by the pen fiasco, rerunning it in my head, but I did pull it together enough to sit down. He held out my pen, giving it back to me.

"Here you go. Looks like we don't have to sign in this time."

I took the pen back, relieved that he hadn't had that much time to inspect its condition. Just then, Derek walked in, and I waved him over. But as soon as I did it, I felt weird—I mean, did Felix want to sit next to me alone? Was I abusing his invitation by extending it to others?

Derek came over, looking a little shocked and unsure about the fact that I was sitting next to Felix. He sat next to me, and I introduced them.

"Hey, Derek. This is Felix. Felix, Derek."

Felix did a little chin-lift thing as an acknowledgment. Derek gave a weak, "Hi."

"So, um, is this your first time auditioning at Oaks?" I asked Felix.

"Yeah, it is. I'm a junior at St. Paul's."

I almost said, "I know," but somehow I stopped myself in time. Apparently, my dignity was slowly making its way back to me.

"The shows at my school are stupid, and I've heard a lot about this theater," he said, looking around admiringly. Derek and I looked around, too, as if we hadn't seen the room until that moment (speaking of "stupid").

It occurred to me that this was the first time that I was in a social situation with Derek and not Jimmy. If Derek and I both made it into the play, we would be spending a lot of time together. And if Jimmy and he broke up, would he quit? After all, the whole reason he'd auditioned was because Jimmy basically forced him to. I snapped out of this little daydream to the horrifying realization that Felix had apparently just asked me something.

Oh, God. What did he just say?

Heaven bless her, Jenny McCafferty picked that moment to start clapping and yelling, "OK, settle down, folks. Let's get started." I gave Felix an apologetic shrug and smile, as if to say, "Gee, I guess I can't answer your question now!"

Note to self: Learn how to follow a conversation.

Sister Mary Alice shooed Jenny offstage and gestured for the kids who were sitting farther away to move closer.

"Welcome and congratulations! You all had splendid auditions last week, and today we are in the final phase of the casting process. Thirty of you have been called back, and eighteen of you will be in the final cast. I don't know about you, but *I'm* a bundle of nerves today." Sister Mary Alice bugged her eyes out and bared her lower teeth in an expression of mock terror. We all laughed—I guess you just had to see it—but it was an uneasy laughter all the same.

She continued. "This is the hardest part of the auditioning process, mostly because there is no way for anyone to prepare for what we're going to do today. I will take you through a series of improvisational acting exercises, because I want to see what spark you can bring to a character. This musical isn't just about looking the part or singing the part. We know you can do that. But beyond how you appear or sound, this play really requires you to take characters from childhood fairy tales—characters everyone already knows—and make the audience connect with them in new, powerful ways." She looked us over, appraising us with her hard stare. "Well. Let's get started, then."

We began by playing a game of Freeze. It's a really basic exercise where two people improvise a scene, and whenever someone else wants to jump in, they yell, "Freeze!" The two actors "freeze" whatever they're doing, and the new person has to replace one of the actors and start an entirely new scene based on how they're physically positioned. Confusing? Don't worry. I'll walk you through it.

So the first people to go were some guy from Cathedral Latin and Maria Kilkenny. You know, the big girl with the amazing voice? Since they were first, Sister Mary Alice gave them the scene, telling them that they were two people who hadn't seen each other for forty years. (I couldn't help but think, Gee, is that what Sister considers normal, at her age? Xiang was definitely having an influence on me.)

"Oh, Hal!" exclaimed Maria, throwing herself at Cathedral Latin Guy and enveloping him in a big hug.

"Uh . . . Janice! It's, uh, been so long!" he exclaimed, obviously alarmed by her sudden attack. He managed to recover a bit and awkwardly began patting her back.

"FREEZE!" yelled a blond guy, and Maria and Cathedral Latin Guy froze in position. The blond guy jumped onstage, and he took the place of Cathedral Latin Guy in the scene. There were some knowing chuckles in the room—people assumed from the hug position that Blondie was about to start some kind of sexual groping scene with Maria.

But instead of patting her back gently, he pounded it as if she were a conga drum. "Spit it out! Come on, Alice, don't choke on me here!" he yelled. She immediately caught on and started gagging and calling for water.

And so on and so forth. At various times, Felix was a narcoleptic cab driver, a televangelist, a brain surgeon, and a burning tree. Derek was a drug addict, a screaming toddler, and half of a horse—luckily, the front half. I was a hyper poodle, a bitchy cheerleader, and an ice sculptor (clever, no?). You know, par for the course. And, actually, it was a great way for me to shake all my nervousness and spastic demeanor around Felix. So it felt as if barely any time had gone by when Sister Mary Alice clapped her hands and said we were moving on to another exercise. I just happened to end up standing next to Felix.

And that's when it happened.

That was the moment he leaned in close and breathed into my ear: "I have to tell you . . . you're really beautiful."

No one had yelled anything, but I couldn't have been more frozen.

O h, boy.

You know how it feels when someone is watching you? Like, I mean, *really watching* you? I don't remember a thing from the rest of the callback audition, except that Felix kept his eyes on me the whole time.

And . . . I liked it.

I mean, that perfectly formed human being was paying attention to—no, he was *transfixed by*—ridiculous, dorky me. We didn't know each other beyond exchanging a few words, but all of a sudden I couldn't focus on anyone else, and he was completely focused on me.

This had obviously never happened to me before, so I had zero idea of how to deal with it. Luckily, when rehersal ended, there was no natural opportunity to talk more, so we each drifted our separate ways.

Oh, God—what if we didn't get cast in the play?

Oh, who was I kidding? He was a shoo-in. But what if I didn't get a part? Would I ever see him again?

If we *did* both get parts . . . what would I say the next time I saw him, at the first rehearsal? What was he doing *right now*? Did he live with that old lady from the mall, presumably his grandmother? What was the rest of his family like?

Was he considering out-of-state colleges? How did his hair smell? What would we name our firstborn?

I know, I know, I'm a crazy person. But these were the kinds of questions I was asking myself all throughout the next day at school.

Xiang demanded the lowdown, every little detail, at lunch, and together we pondered all the different potential outcomes of this new Felix bombshell. I was obviously really excited that this gorgeous guy—a *junior*, no less—thought I was beautiful and had said it to me, but . . . now what?

Or was I just being crazy over a simple, harmless compliment?

Not when I thought about the way he looked at me, no.

Unfortunately, I think the Felix discussion only made Xiang more unsettled, since she had the orchestra audition after school, and Parker was definitely coming. She was determined to take Kirby's advice about starting a covert romance, parents be damned. In a way, we were in the same boat—we both knew our guys were sort of interested, but . . . what was the next step? We decided she would come over to my house for a "study session" later on to recap on whatever happened after school.

And, frankly, it was nice to have my own romantic drama—at last!

As an added bonus, this whole Felix thing was a welcome distraction from my nervousness over the results of the callback audition. Jenny had said that the final cast list would be posted "in the next couple of days," so I spent all day wrapped up in my own anticipation, not really seeing or hearing anything around me (unless it pertained to Felix, of course). And you can bet your bottom dollar that I was frantically checking my inbox between every one of my classes.

And about every 3.5 seconds once I got home.

My mom was out, but Dad was cooking up a storm in the kitchen. I brought my laptop in and opened it up at the counter island with a heavy, dramatic sigh.

"Hey, what's shakin'?" he asked, chopping away.

I pulled my hair back and held it with one fist in a ponytail. "They're supposed to post the cast list any moment now. Is there any way I can add a noise alert to my inbox, so I can stop staring at the screen?" I wiggled my way onto one of the counter stools.

"Um . . . not that I know of. Maybe check under Settings. Is there a particular role you're hoping to get?"

"No, not really. I mean, a *big* role would be nice, but since I'm only a freshman, I'm not expecting much. I just hope I get in. And my friends, too," I added, thinking of a certain, brand-new, older, *hottie* friend.

"Well, you'll definitely get cast—don't you worry," he said, adding onions to the saucepan. "And if you don't get cast, it's not the end of the world."

Easy for him to say!

"Oh, you got my voice mail earlier that Xiang is coming over for dinner, right?" I asked, momentarily mesmerized by the hissing and popping coming from the stove.

"Not a problem. We got lots of beans and peppers in our local-farms box this week, so there will be chili aplenty—in fact, I'm hoping we have lots of leftovers. It always tastes better the next day, when all the juices have really settled in. It gets thicker when it cools, you know, and that gives it the perfect texture for . . ."

Yeah, yeah. Whatever. I turned back to my screen and opened up a search engine. I typed in *Felix Peroni* and waded through a bunch of stuff on some Argentinian viola player.

Then I came across the public listing for his Facebook profile.

It was definitely my Felix in the picture, even though he had cropped it weirdly, so it only showed the top half of his head. The page showed a few of his friends, and spiky-haired Matt Brezinski was one of them. I couldn't access any real info, though, since we hadn't "friended" each other. Would it be weird if I suddenly sent him a friend request? I mean, we hit it off at callbacks, so . . . not weird, right?

My dad tapped a glass with his spoon, and the ringing brought me back into reality. I realized I must have spaced out for quite a while, actually. "What, may I ask, is so interesting that you can't answer a simple question?"

Caught! "Oh, um, nothing—"

And then, as they say, I was saved by the bell.

"Oh! That must be Xiang." I slapped my laptop shut and sprinted to the front door.

"Salutations, my beatific broccolini!" Jimmy threw himself upon me, smothering me in a hug, while Oliver slinked inside behind him.

"Hey, guys—to what do I owe this unexpected pleasure?"

"We have great news!" Jimmy grabbed my hand and pulled me back into the kitchen, Oliver still trailing behind.

My dad looked up from the stove when they walked in. "Oh, are there two more of you for dinner, then?"

"Oh, no, they—" I started, but Jimmy cut me off.

"If it's not too much trouble, Mr. Sullivan, we'd love to stay!"

Excuse me? Jimmy hates my dad's veggie food almost as much as I do! I mouthed, "Seriously?" at him, and he responded with a half shrug.

"Oh, it's no trouble at all, Jimmy. Looks like we'll have just enough with this chili. And for the thousandth time, call me Doug." Ugh. I mentally hurled a Molotov cocktail at my dad. Sorry, but you're a *dad*, not a *Doug*.

Hee, but I love that Jimmy still can't bring himself to call him that, no matter how much my dad tries.

"And who is this?" My dad gave Oliver the paternal once-over, as if he was somehow telling Oliver to keep his hands off me. Oh, my clueless father.

"*This* is Oliver," I said. I grabbed my laptop in one hand and Oliver's hand in the other and dragged him (and therefore Jimmy) out of the kitchen. "Call us when Xiang comes!"

Up in my room, I tossed the laptop onto the desk and flopped onto my bed. Jimmy flung himself next to me, while Oliver perched carefully on a corner of the mattress, as if he didn't quite know what to do with himself in a girl's bed-room.

"So. What's the big news?" I asked.

Jimmy slapped two hands onto one knee. "Well. You know how we don't spend enough time together now that you're off at that nunnery, and Oliver and I didn't make it to the callbacks?"

"That particular situation has not escaped my notice."

Jimmy rolled his eyes. "Bee-yatch, a simple 'yes' would be nice. Anyway, we're going to join your play."

"Um . . . have you murdered off the competition?"

He waved his arms over himself and Oliver, magician-style. "Nope. You are looking at two newly minted assistant stage managers."

"Shut. Up."

"No, really. Apparently, no one from your school signed up, so the stage manager let us do it."

"Shut up."

"I'm serious."

"Shut up."

"OK, stop saying that."

"Really? *Really* really? You guys are willing to deal with Jenny McCafferty just to spend more time with *me*?" My eyes went back and forth between Jimmy and Oliver like an Olympic Ping-Pong ball. They settled on Oliver.

"Well, you and Derek," Oliver said. "He insisted we do *something* in the play, since he's gonna have to be there."

I gasped. *"The list!"*

I physically launched myself toward my laptop on the desk. "They sent it out? Derek got a role? *I* got a role?" Oh, curse the distracting power of Facebook! I clicked on my inbox tab, and, *voilà*, there it was.

Maria Kilkenney—Witch, Kate O'Day—Cinderella, Felix Peroni—Wolf / Cinderella's Prince, Derek Mylvaganam—Baker, Martha Sullivan—Little Red Riding Hood!

OMG!!

Just at that moment, my dad called us down to dinner because Xiang had arrived.

As we trudged down the stairs, I could not stop beaming, and a song started playing somewhere in the back of my head: *Felix and Marty, sitting in a tree, K-I-S-S-I-N-G*...

Spill, sister," I said the minute my bedroom door closed.

Xiang, Oliver, Jimmy, and I had retreated up to my room after dinner. My mom and dad were downstairs clearing the dishes (What? I had guests to entertain!), so we slipped upstairs to get the scoop on what, if anything, had happened between Xiang and Parker at their orchestra rehearsal.

"Yeah, but hurry, because my dad will be here to pick me up any minute," said Oliver, checking his watch. "I can't *wait* for my birthday in a couple of months," he muttered.

"Oooh, then you'll be our very own personal chauffeur!" I purred.

"I'll take you anywhere and everywhere you wanna go," he said, grinning in that way that really highlights his jaw-line.

"Hello? You wanna hear this or not?" Xiang barked at us.

"Yes! Yes! Do tell!"

Xiang's eyes shone, and she looked like she was about to explode into a million pieces.

"It. Was. *Awesome.*"

We leaned forward, grinning stupidly with anticipation.

Xiang lowered her voice to a whisper. "We hooked up in one of the classrooms."

Silence.

"Hooked up—you mean, kissed?" Jimmy finally said.

"Yeah . . . and a bit more than that," she replied, grinning widely.

Jimmy swallowed hard, and Oliver looked a little green.

Me? I knew Xiang too well to fall for that. Xiang? Making out with some guy she barely knows? At our nun-run school? Please.

"Riiiiight. And now I suppose you're pregnant with his baby," I said, rolling my eyes.

Xiang sighed. "Well, not a possibility yet," she said, "but I could totally see us going a lot further in the near future. I mean, *I* want to."

She looked really serious. My disbelief started to fissure.

"Xiang. You're kidding. I know you're kidding."

"Nope. We totally hit it off, and all the awkwardness just melted away. It just seemed so natural, the way we were talking and connecting, and then all of a sudden we were in this classroom, and . . ." She looked at each of us with that bright, shining expression she'd had all throughout dinner (now that I thought about it). "Well, you know."

Oh, boy. She really wasn't kidding.

"But . . . um, how . . . ," I sputtered, by now completely bewildered. Shock doesn't even begin to describe the feeling. I mean, I knew that some fifteen-year-olds supposedly start having sex, but somehow the idea just seemed really abstract and far away, something that happened to other people I didn't *actually know*. Jimmy and Derek were probably doing *stuff,* but he and I hadn't ever talked about it. Oh, God—what *had* they done together?

And here I was all day, obsessing over the fact that some guy had *said* he thought I was beautiful, while everyone else apparently was going at each other like . . . like . . . rabbits in heat!

"I dunno, it just kind of happened," Xiang said breezily. "I mean, we snuck into the room after the audition to talk, and then the next thing I knew . . ." She shrugged.

"Man, Kirby's gonna regret not having been here for *this,*" Oliver breathed.

"I know. It's crazy, right?" squealed Xiang, clearly delighted to be the center of attention. "It's weird how it's changed the whole dynamic with Parker. I mean, before I was all jittery around him, but now it's just, like, I'm not hesitant at all. I just want to grab him and, like, you know?"

No, we don't know, I wanted to say. She was really pissing me off, and I wasn't exactly sure why.

At least she wasn't using that high, babyish voice anymore.

Just then we heard a car pull into the driveway, and Oliver sprang up to look out the window.

"Yup, that's Dad. I gotta roll. Congratulations again on getting the part, Marty. You deserve it." He gave me a solid hug. What a cutie.

Then he turned to Xiang uncertainly. "And . . . uh, congratulations, I guess."

Jimmy jumped up, too. "Oooh, look at the time. Sorry, ladies, I have to finish my chem lab report for tomorrow. Later!"

He gave us ironic air kisses, and then—*whoosh*—they were gone.

I wouldn't have guessed it, but apparently my gay boys weren't terribly comfortable when girls started talking about hooking up.

Xiang pulled out her cell phone and started tapping away. I got up and watched through the window as Oliver walked to the red Honda idling in the driveway.

Which classroom had Xiang picked for her little *liaison*? Oh, man—Mr. Dartagnon's room? No, too far away from the auditions. Eww, didn't Xiang say Sister Mary Alice had *couches* in her classroom?

Outside, Oliver said something to his dad, who had gotten out of the car, and they both cracked up laughing. His dad had cropped gray hair and a goatee; actually, he was pretty handsome for an old guy. I could see where Oliver got his looks from.

Oliver opened the driver's side door and dropped into the seat, then carefully backed the car out of the driveway. Like me, Jimmy just stood there, off to the side, watching Oliver maneuver the Honda. Then Jimmy waved up at me before switching on a flashlight and heading into the backyard, toward the woods.

"So," I said, turning to Xiang, who was still tapping at her phone. "What's your plan?"

"Plan?"

"I mean, what's next? How is this whole Blarker thing going to work?" I could feel an edge in my own voice, and I hated the way I sounded: critical, aggressive.

Xiang's glow-y aura dimmed a bit. "Um, I dunno. I guess we'll just figure it out. We see each other every weekend at CYO. Plus, there weren't that many people auditioning for the musical's orchestra today, so we'll probably both get in."

I realized we hadn't even discussed her audition at all, not even at dinner.

"You're texting him right now, aren't you? You're obsessed."

Xiang smirked dismissively and kept on tapping away. I got the distinct impression that she didn't think I could understand, nonsmoker and non-hooking-up virgin that I am.

"Fine, whatever," I said wearily. Xiang's phone buzzed as I left to retrieve my book bag from downstairs. I glanced back to see her sprawled over my bed, a stupid grin spread over her face as she read the new message.

Later, after Xiang had gone home, I called Jimmy.

"Xiang's not one to take things slow, huh?" I asked, staring at my ceiling from the exact same spot where Xiang had been sending pornographic text messages an hour ago. (OK, I don't *know* that they were pornographic.)

Jimmy whistled. "Yeah, I was definitely not expecting that!"

"Yeah . . ."

"Kind of like you and what's-his-face," Jimmy said teasingly. He was referring to Felix, obviously—I had called Jimmy the minute I left the audition yesterday to tell him all about Felix and his . . . whatever that was. Compliment? Courtship attempt?

"Oh, please. I have no idea what's actually going on with Felix. If anything. I mean, maybe he was just joking, or having a stroke or something."

"Uh-huh," Jimmy said, and I didn't have to see him to know the skeptical expression on his face.

OK, time to put *him* on the defensive. "So how's it going with Derek?"

Jimmy sighed loudly.

"That bad?" I asked, joking.

"What? No, that was a happy sigh! A very happy sigh! I'm smiling!"

"Aww, that's sweet," I said mechanically. (Look, there's only so much enthusiasm I can be expected to show. Derek's nice and all, but you can't blame me for not being over the moon about him taking my Jimmy away from me.)

"All this romance in the air," Jimmy mused. "Even Kirby's got *something* going on, even if it is in cyberspace."

"I guess the only odd one out in our little group is Oliver," I said. "Poor guy. He seemed pretty heartbroken the other week, talking about his ex."

"Well, as a matter of fact, I've heard that the tide is turning for him," Jimmy said.

"Really? He's got a crush?" I asked.

"Yup, that's what Derek says. But Oliver swore Derek to absolute secrecy, so don't you *dare* breathe a word of this to anyone. Derek would kill me if he knew I was spilling the beans—or at least the one tiny bean that he spilled to me. I mean, he would kill me if Oliver didn't kill him first for telling me. And he isn't telling Kirby, because Kirby would totally blab about it."

"OK, now you're making my head hurt," I said. "Honestly, who am I gonna tell? And there's no way I even know this person."

"Well, don't mention anything about a crush to *Oliver,* for starters," Jimmy said, yawning. "Or Derek. Or anyone. But anyway, it's time to hang up. I seriously need to do this chemistry shit."

"Yeah, OK," I murmured gloomily.

"Yeah, OK?' You sound kind of down. Is everything all right?"

"Yeah, everything's fine," I said, sitting up. "I'm just tired. Sorry. Go, go. Learn some science! We'll talk later. Are you guys coming to the first rehearsal on Thursday?"

"I don't think Mistress McCafferty will let us miss *any* of the full-cast rehearsals, so don't worry—you'll be seeing an awful lot of me and Oliver."

"Aww, you guys are the best. You know I love you, right?"

"Love you, too, babe. G'night, cucumber cutie."

"G'night, my pretty potato."

The next morning at school I received an unexpected gift from Jenny McCafferty.

She had created a Facebook group for *Into the Woods* ("SIGN UP FOR IMPORTANT LAST-MINUTE EMERGENCY UPDATES!!!"), so I was given the *perfect* excuse to friend Felix in order to conduct some deep research on him. So I sent off my friend request to him (and everyone else, too, to not appear too stalkerish) and waited.

And waited.

And waited some more.

Honestly, I was getting sick of checking my various devices, especially since I had spent all of *yesterday* checking my inbox for the cast list.

By the end of the day, everyone else had signed up to the group and answered my friend requests. And I mean everyone. Ferchrissake, *Mrs. Murray* signed up, and now we were online BFFs. *Don't they have computers at St. Paul's? Or phones?*

At least Felix didn't join the Facebook group and ignore my invitation—could you just imagine if *that* had happened?

"It is very uncool of him," Xiang agreed as we walked toward the parking lot, where my mom was waiting in the car.

But Xiang's distant, moony expression made me think she wasn't even really listening; she and Parker had been officially notified that they were both in the show's orchestra, so there were definitely going to be some hot times in the orchestra pit this fall. Eww. Meanwhile, I was *supposed* to be all psyched and giddy over getting the Little Red Riding Hood part.

A crap day.

The next morning was Thursday, the first rehearsal day, and it was the first time since coming to Our Lady that I really spent time examining myself in the mirror and gussying up before heading off to school. I mean, I would be interacting with boys, and now that Felix had said I was beautiful, I had a reputation to uphold! And if his lack of online activity meant that he wasn't that into me, maybe he'd think twice?

I managed to get to Jerry Hall a bit early. When I walked into Room A, one of three rehearsal spaces tucked away behind the auditorium, I quickly learned that I didn't have anything to worry about: Felix was instantly at my side, breathing into my ear.

"Hiya."

Suddenly the world went from an angry, dirty magenta to a cool, sparkly white.

I turned, smiling. "Hi, there."

His perfect row of upper teeth was absolutely hypnotic.

"I've been thinking about you."

Ohhh, meltiness . . .

"Really?" I exhaled.

Then I suddenly remembered I was mad at him. "Well, you know there are these newfangled things called computers, not to mention phones? Those strange, thin boxes that glow?"

He looked away, across the room, still smiling that killer smile. "Oh, you mean Facebook. I got your invitation in my e-mail, but I can't get my Facebook account to work. I think someone hijacked my password and changed it. Probably one of my buds at St. Paul's." He grabbed my hand and held it, entwining his fingers with mine. "But were you thinking about me?"

I was surprised by the sudden physical contact and a little embarrassed by the question. What am I supposed to say: "Oh, honey. *Incessantly*"? I mean, I couldn't say that!

I decided to play it coy. "Maaaybe . . ."

His grin grew even wider. "Sweet. 'Cause I can't get you out of my head."

I just blushed in response. Never in my life had anyone ever said anything remotely like that to me, and the fact that it was coming from the most beautiful person on the planet was just . . . unreal. He was so forward, so direct; it was unnerving.

Clearly, I was dreaming. I was asleep in my bedroom on Iroquois Trail, drooling on my pillow and strangling a pink Care Bear with my twisted sheets.

Or was I?

Suddenly he pulled his hand away, stepped back, and

kinda slumped, looking down at the floor. "Sorry, I'm probably freaking you out. I mean, I'm freaking me out!"

"No, no," I said, putting a hand on his upper arm.

There was a muscle there. A proper, wonderful muscle.

"It's just—I dunno. I just feel like we have a connection," he said. "You probably think I'm nuts." He brushed a fallen lock of hair back from his eyes and peered at me.

"I don't think you're nuts." We just looked at each other for a long moment, and I was tongue-tied. I mean, what was the appropriate response? Seriously. Is there something—anything—to say? Something about the play, the weather, politics, sports . . .?

"Actually, I'm a liar. You definitely are nuts."

Did I just say that? Did I just completely kill the moment by trying to be coy and funny? Oh, God. A classic Marty misfire.

But it wasn't. He very gently leaned forward and placed his lips against mine.

Reality came back hard and fast as I broke away from the kiss and saw Jimmy staring at us. I thought we were alone in the room, but he must have just walked in, holding a pile of identical paperback books. He looked shocked. Felix ran a hand through his hair and kind of stepped back from me, flustered.

A wave of shame washed over me. I mean, I *knew* I had nothing to be ashamed of, but I still felt the feeling throughout my body. Jimmy was my, like, soulmate, and to have him see me . . . I dunno, it just felt super-awkward. But I didn't have time to process everything, because Jenny barged in, clapping a hand against her clipboard and shouting "Listen up!" to a bunch of people walking in behind her. Oliver stumbled in, too, holding more of those paperbacks in his arms.

Then I turned back toward Felix, who locked eyes with mine and smiled a small, secret smile, and I felt something unfurl within me.

"OK, guys, here are your scripts!" Jenny was saying. "Grab one and make sure to write your name on the inside cover—we don't want them getting all mixed up once you've started highlighting and taking notes on blocking. We're still missing a few folks, but Sister Mary Alice and Mrs. Murray are on their way, so let's be ready when they come in. Grab yourself a chair from the back, and let's arrange them in four rows, facing this wall. On this show, we're going to hit the ground running!" Jenny looked around the room with bright eyes.

God, she was irritating.

I pivoted toward Felix and did a quick "Hit the ground running!" McCafferty imitation, and he chuckled soundlessly in response. As I turned back, I thought I saw Jenny meet my glance, but she quickly looked down and spread the wobbly piles of scripts into two fans across the table. Everyone moseyed over toward them, and Oliver gave me a slow wink as he handed me mine. Jimmy was standing next to him, and I tried to make eye contact, dying to know what he was thinking about me and Felix. Unfortunately, he was too busy checking off people's names on Jenny's clipboard.

Then everyone lumbered over to grab metal folding chairs from a rolling rack by the far wall. The door opened, and Mrs. Murray backed into the room, pulling a rickety, old-school TV stand into the room. Sister Mary Alice emerged from behind it, and she helped guide the television toward the front of the room. "Oh, heavens, this is heavy. Thank you, Nancy."

Jenny ushered Jimmy and Oliver to the back of the room with her usual officiousness. Felix was seated in the row just in front of me, and we exchanged a few shy glances before he finally turned to face forward.

I leaned back in my chair and looked around the room at the other actors. Maria Kilkenny was whispering away with this tall girl named Penelope, who was cast as the Baker's Wife, so Derek would be having lots of scenes with her. (Actually, the Baker's Wife is probably the biggest role in the whole musical, but people always seem to forget about it, because she's not a famous fairy-tale character.) Then there was a clump of three guys—Jason, Kirk, and Foster—who would be playing the Narrator, Rapunzel's Prince, and Jack. They were all from a town not too far from Our Lady of the Oaks, and so far they were pretty shy around all us girls. Glamorous Kate O'Day, who was Cinderella, was sitting right in the front, notebook and pen ready. Short and friendly Mr. Gonzalez, one of the cooks from the cafeteria, had been recruited by Sister Mary Alice to play

Cinderella's Father, since he only had a couple of lines in the whole play and it wasn't worth bringing in some guy from another school for the role. This would be the last time we saw him, though, until dress rehearsals. He hovered near the back of the room, just in front of the gaggle of three girls—Jenna, Madison, and Emma—who would be playing Cinderella's Stepmother and Stepsisters. They were also with Chloe, who would be playing Jack's Mother. I was sitting next to Daisy, who was playing Cinderella's Mother and the King's Guard. (Normally the guard is a male role, but, well, it's a girls' school, and there's not much to either role.) I smiled at her as people settled in, and she beamed back at me. "This is so exciting!" she whispered.

"I know, right?"

This play was going to *rock*.

More likely, I was feeling all dreamy because my lips were numb with prickly pleasure. In fact, I could swear they were actually swelling—is that a thing? Does that happen to everyone, every time they kiss? Are people walking around in a constant state of lip puffiness? And I couldn't help staring at the back of Felix's head. Who knew the back of someone's head could be so interesting?

Sister Mary Alice popped a DVD into the player on the TV stand and finally turned to address us. "Ah, my intrepid crew of thespians!"

Meanwhile, Mrs. Murray double-fisted the remote controls, trying to get the screen to work. I looked back at Jimmy, who made a funny, bewildered face at me. In response, I covered my eyes with one hand, in mock shame.

OK, so things weren't *that* weird between us because of the kiss.

"This will be your easiest rehearsal," Sister continued, heading over to the light switch. "You don't have to do a thing. Today we're just going to watch the original Broadway production from 1987 so we know exactly what we've gotten ourselves into." She chuckled. "On second thought, this might be the most difficult rehearsal. I assure you, I will *not* accept any resignations after the screening."

The lights dimmed, the show began, and I sat there, watching the blue light of the television caress the silhouette of the head in front of me.

Lights, camera, *action.*

15

So then, after the movie/rehearsal ended, Felix and I went into an empty classroom and had hot monkey sex.

snort

Yeah, not quite. Sister Mary Alice turned off the TV once the credits came up, then started going through the different roles, explaining what she saw to be the main challenges for each actor.

"Martha," she eventually said, turning to me, "I think the role of Little Red Riding Hood is one of the hardest."

Oh, crap.

She continued, "True, she does seem pretty simple and straightforward, and she gets to deliver some of the funniest lines. But unlike all the other roles, Little Red doesn't have a clear trajectory that makes sense to me. Normally, a character wants something, so they go and get it. Along the way they make choices, have regrets, learn something about themselves and the world. But in your case, you're stuck between being a child and an adult."

I swallowed. The way she kept saying *you* made it all sound weirdly personal.

"I'm not sure what you want, other than the occasional

sweet," Sister continued, shaking her head. "After your encounter with the wolf, you learn about naïveté and protection, so you do seem to grow up. But in the second act you become orphaned, and you're still very vulnerable. The trick for you will be to make that believable. I want the audience to understand that even when you seem most sophisticated and most confident, you're actually totally outside of your comfort zone, that it's all just bluster. That's the only way you'll have our sympathy later on, when you really need help. No easy feat for any actor."

Then, after what seemed like an unusually long moment of me nodding back at her, Sister turned to Maria Kilkenny. "Now, the Witch is a whole other story . . ."

OK, I thought to myself, I can do this.

And, actually, I was eager for the real rehearsals to start. Acting is fun! I mean, I think it's really weird that as kids we're constantly pretending to be someone or something else, and then suddenly we all grow up, and the only place we can keep playing is onstage. Doesn't that seem . . . wrong? I feel like everyone should be in theater.

Sister continued with her character breakdowns, and when she got to Derek, he tensed up and flushed.

"The Baker, in my view, is the hero of this show," she said, clasping and reclasping her hands. "Yes, he ends up protecting the children and defeating the Giant's Wife. But really it's his struggle with right and wrong that makes him heroic to me. And, like all of us, he doesn't always get it right."

Sister paused and took a deep breath. "Now, Derek."

Derek swallowed audibly. "I know you're not used to being onstage. But you have a great talent, and I don't want you to hide your light under a bushel."

(I think Sister may have forgotten that people at secular schools don't necessarily get Bible references, but if Derek was confused, he didn't let on.)

She continued. "Your challenge will be to *use* your insecurity about being onstage. I want you to embrace it and channel it into your character. The Baker is insecure about everything, from the second scene onward. Everything he thought was right and good and proper is turned upside down. His whole world becomes upended with disappointment and betrayal and grief. And he, like us, comes out stronger at the end. He learns, and we as an audience learn along with him. So, in many ways the play rests on your shoulders."

Derek couldn't have looked more pained. Sister chuckled at the sight of him and walked over to pat him on the shoulder. "Don't you worry, you'll be fine. We'll make sure of it."

When "rehearsal" was over, and everyone was busy folding their chairs and returning them to the racks along the back wall, Felix pulled me aside, far from the others.

"About before, I'm sorry if I—"

"What? No, don't be sorry!" I said quickly. "I mean, there's really nothing to be sorry about. It was all good." *All good?* "You know, it was, well, a moment. Or whatever."

Oh, Marty, shut up, just shut up. But I couldn't stop: "Really, it's no biggie."

You know, like I make out with cute boys *all the time*. Make-out Marty, that's my name!

Felix looked up at the ceiling with a pained expression, then said, "It's just that maybe it wasn't a good idea."

WHAT?

Oh, God. My scalp tensed up, preparing for The Worst Thing Ever Imaginable.

He must have seen my terrified expression, because he stepped closer and put a hand on my arm. "No, no, no, no, no, don't get me wrong! It was a *great* idea! I just . . . I think we should try to keep this between us. Under wraps."

"I wasn't going to . . . I mean . . . ," I stammered.

"Plays like this one, they can be really intense. And I don't want people to be weirded out that we're, like, *you know*, and to be talking about us all the time."

I opened my mouth to say something—honestly, I had no idea what it would be—but he rushed in again. "Don't get me wrong! I want us to, *you know*. But maybe not, like, in everyone's faces. I'm just worried that it'll make things strange and complicated. I've seen that happen before, and the whole fishbowl thing can really screw it up. You know?"

He looked at me searchingly, almost desperately, and I felt my whole body unclench. After the awkwardness of seeing Jimmy see us kiss, it wasn't like I was looking forward to more PDA. "No worries," I said, relaxing into an easy smile.

"I just think we've got something here, and I don't want to mess it up." He didn't seem convinced that I understood him, and it was touching to see how worried he looked.

"Felix. It's OK," I said. Now it was my turn to reach out and rub his arm (the muscle!). "What we do together, well, it's nobody's business."

Now, how cool was I? *Finally*, for once I had said the exact right thing to him. And it was true: This was nobody's sweet business but *ours*.

Then we just sort of grinned at each other for another lingering second before Felix turned and walked off.

Moments later, Jimmy materialized in front of me. "You," he exclaimed, wild-eyed. "And . . . *that guy!*" Jimmy flailed his other arm toward the door.

I snapped my fingers in a sassy arc. "Damn straight."

He was giving me an appraising look, clearly impressed. "I can*not* believe this. Seriously. Well played, Sullivan. Ten points for Gryffindor!"

"But, Jimmy, you can't tell anyone. Swear."

"What? What do you mean?"

"I really don't want people talking about it. Trust me, it'll make the whole play weird if everyone knows we're together. So keep it to yourself. Got it?"

Jimmy huffed and rolled his eyes.

"I'm serious. Not even Derek."

I could see the wheels turning in Jimmy's head. Could he and I still have secrets, or would he run to tell Derek any little thing I told him? I was testing how he would handle this, and he knew it. And he knew I knew it. And I knew he knew I—yeah, well, you get the picture.

"Fine," he finally said, waving the issue away with his hand. "Whatever. But I am still in *total shock* over this."

"I know," I said—OK, squealed.

Jimmy put his arm around my shoulders as we walked out of Rehearsal Room A.

"Aww, my little Marty. They grow up so fast, don't they!"

"Ugh, finally, it's Friday!" Xiang's peach-colored plastic lunch tray clattered onto the table across from me.

"I know. It's been such a long, crazy week, hasn't it?" I asked. I mean, it really had been, what with the callbacks on Monday, the anxiety over getting cast in the musical, Xiang going practically nympho, then the Big Kiss last night—how much more could happen?

Xiang eyed me, noting the chipper tone in my voice. Suddenly her hand slammed down onto the table, rattling the tableware. "You didn't!" she exclaimed.

I snapped a celery stick in two. "Did. Too."

Xiang made a high-pitched "eep" sound.

Yes, it's true: This was turning out to be the worst-kept secret ever. But I figured, what's one more person? I mean, Xiang had totally overshared her own romance, and she totally knew that Felix was into me anyway, so it was only fair to reciprocate.

"Oh. My. God." She shook her head. "Wow."

"Hey, now—don't be getting the wrong idea," I said, suddenly unnerved by the smirk she was giving me. "We kissed. That's all."

Her smirk stayed firmly in place. "Well, well, well. You wanton slut."

"Thank you," I said regally, waving a half celery stick at her in a twirling, bowing motion. "But it's very hush-hush, since we don't want to freak out the rest of the cast. So *no telling anyone.*"

"Ooooooh, a *secret* romance! The plot thickens!"

I let myself do a little bouncy dance in my chair. "Can you *believe* it? *Felix friggin' Peroni!* Mall Guy! Things like this aren't supposed to happen in real life!"

"So he'll make an honest woman out of you after the play closes? You'll make it official and announce it to the world?"

"Yeah, I guess. Although, honestly, I don't think this secret is one we'll be able to keep for long."

Xiang snorted. "No, apparently not."

"You shut up. But I can't stop thinking about him! I think I totally failed the algebra quiz this morning. I can't focus."

Xiang nodded in sympathy. "Yeah, you probably shouldn't operate heavy machinery, either."

"Right. Noted." I sighed, still swaying happily in my seat. "So. You comin' tonight?"

That night Kirby was . . . being Kirby.

He was driving us—me, Xiang, and Oliver—to God-knows-where for God-knows-what reason. The original

plan was for *all* of us to hang out, Jimmy and Derek included, but then they dropped out at the last minute to go do
boyfriend-y things.

And when Jimmy had called to announce that they were
dropping out of the plans, I'd assumed that Kirby and Oliver
would want to do their own thing.

"Oh, no," Jimmy had said hurriedly. "You have to go. Derek
insists that you go, or he'll feel bad about ruining it for
everyone else. He was crazy-adamant about it."

"Well, then, come along!"

"Marty, come on. I need to spend time with Derek."

No, you don't, I wanted to say. You need to spend time
with me! But Jimmy was doing the whole assistant-stage-
manager thing, and he'd passed my little loyalty test about
keeping Felix secret, so I couldn't exactly argue with him
about his commitment to our friendship.

"You wouldn't want me to show up every time you meet
up with *Felix*," he said.

OK, that was another good point. (Although, technically
speaking, that was exactly what was already happening.)

"And, anyway," he continued, "Kirby and Oliver are really
fun! I don't see why I'm even having to convince you. You'll
have a great time."

So this was going to be the first time Xiang and I were
going out with *friends* of friends. Like, without Jimmy as a
connection, it felt totally weird getting into a car with two
older guys from a completely different part of the Cleveland
area. OK, they weren't *random* guys, as we had hung out a

couple times before. But, still. Thank goodness they were gay; otherwise it would have totally felt like a date.

So it didn't ease any of the awkwardness that Kirby refused to tell us (Oliver, too!) where we were going; he just gave us explicit instructions to bring "sexy-hot" clothes. We feared he was taking us to a strip club or a sex shop or something. Xiang and I both slipped out of our parent-friendly sweats as soon as we got into the car. (My parents gave me a suspicious look as we left the house "to go to Jimmy's"—they must have noticed the odd lumps in the sweats—but they didn't say anything.) Kirby kept smirking and humming along to the dance radio station as we tried to coax the destination out of him. Eventually, we pulled into the parking lot of what looked to be a warehouse.

Xiang was the first to see the sign. "Bowling? *Hells* no."

"Ah, ah, ah," Kirby said, pulling into a spot. "*Disco* bowling. Don't be talkin' smack about Ohio's favorite pastime. It's a very enriching and enjoyable sport."

He took the key out of the ignition and proceeded to put on mirrored aviator sunglasses. "Best to try to blend with the locals as much as we can," he explained. Then he flashed a wicked smile. "Plus, my uncle owns this place, so I think we'll be able to score some pitchers of beer."

"And there we have it," Oliver said, chuckling. "I knew there was something."

"This is what I'm wearing this tiny skirt for? Why 'sexy-hot'?" I asked, already dreading the looks I'd be getting from fat old men inside.

Kirby looked me up and down. "Darling, you should *always* look hot. More to the point, I need you ladies to look as old as possible. For the beer, and, um, *technically speaking*, I'm not supposed to be driving more than one passenger who is under twenty-one. Mum's the word."

I stuck my tongue out at him (mature, right?) and climbed out of the car. I self-consciously stretched down my tube skirt. I'd only bought the skirt to wear over skinny jeans—very Scandinavian chic!—but tonight I figured that, since my legs were miraculously bruise-less (and clean-shaven!), I'd let them roam free.

Inside, "Shake Your Groove Thing" was blasting, and the place was dark, lit only with the purplish glow of black lights. The bowling alley had clearly seen better days—the plastic veneer on all the benches and counters was flaking off—and the disco theme was only halfheartedly embraced. There was a mirror ball turning unsteadily in the middle of the room, and there was a sad wisp of fog sputtering out of a smoke machine in the corner.

"Wow, this is, uh, groovy," Xiang mumbled.

We each got our bowling shoes (is it weird that I thought mine were really cute, even if they had been worn by thousands of people since the late '90s?), and, true to his word, Kirby got us a couple of pitchers of beer.

"Aww, man, if only I had my driver's license now, you wouldn't have to stay sober tonight," said Oliver, patting Kirby on the back.

"Don't underestimate me, man," Kirby said, pulling a

thermos out of his backpack. He poured half a pitcher into it. "There's always the after-party at home."

And, well, we had a blast. We really did. We split into two teams: me and Oliver against Xiang and Kirby. We sucked at the bowling, but it was fun to mock and psych out one another. Actually, Oliver wasn't that bad—relatively speaking —so he coached me on getting the ball to roll *all the way down* the lane.

"You just gotta watch where you're going, keep your eyes on the pins. That's it."

Or not so much. Another gutter ball.

Between bowls, Xiang and Kirby would huddle on their side and get really engrossed in a private conversation. At first I assumed they were just being competitive and talking about bowling, but when I passed closer by after totally missing the pins (yet again), I overheard a few things, and it was clear that they were talking about sex stuff. I was glad that Xiang and Kirby were hitting it off, but I couldn't help but feel rebuffed. I mean, I was supposed to be her sex-talk friend, not Kirby! Especially now that I had locked lips with a boy myself!

But then the beer started setting in, and my annoyance began to fade. Honestly, I didn't want to hear about Xiang and Parker's future sex life, and Oliver was keeping me extremely entertained. I couldn't stop laughing about how freaky he looked in the black light, all eye whites and teeth. (Nice teeth on that boy. Like a sugar-free gum commercial— like Felix.)

"Wait, hold on. I think you're swinging it wrong." Oliver came over and guided my arm from behind. "You've got to release the ball when you're just about . . . there."

I tried it on the next attempt—and I actually knocked down three pins!

(Hey, now. Be nice. It was my first time bowling.)

I screamed and launched myself onto Oliver, giving him a great big bear hug.

(OK, first time bowling *in years*. Two, to be exact.)

I gave Oliver a wet, exaggerated smooch on his cheek, which had the hilarious effect of making him turn bright red. Even when lit by black light.

The beer also totally helped in making us better bowlers (or so it seemed), so Kirby started demanding compensation points for his handicap of total sobriety. We gave them to him but then took them away when his last turn ended up in a strike.

"An outrage!" he claimed, but he and Xiang won anyway.

The loss was totally my fault.

Damn gutter balls.

When Xiang and I eventually got home, wayyyy late (she had managed to score permission to sleep over, an Exciting Development), we were acting much more drunk than our blood-alcohol levels would indicate. I'm sure my parents could hear us banging around and giggling madly, but thankfully they didn't bother to investigate.

Just as we were both falling asleep, I turned to Xiang.

"Do you realize that I haven't thought about Felix all

night?" (OK, that was a lie. But it wasn't nearly as often as I had, say, earlier in the day.)

Xiang rubbed her eyes, smudging a last bit of eyeliner that she hadn't gotten off in the bathroom. "Really?"

"Do you think that's a good thing or a bad thing?"

She yawned. "Good thing. Shows you're an independent woman."

For moment, I gazed at the shadows on my ceiling cast by trees from outside. The thinnest parts, the branches, looked like tributaries of a dark river, draining into ever-wider courses.

I looked over to see Xiang typing into her cell. "Are you seriously texting Parker right now? Again? You can barely keep your eyes open."

"No, I'm not, if you must know," she said. "I'm texting Kirby."

Kirby? Her new best friend Kirby? I knew it didn't make any sense, but somehow I felt that it was deeply unfair that she was becoming all buddy-buddy with someone she knew 100 percent through me.

OK, even in my grumpy, somewhat drunken state, I knew I was being ridiculous. I mean, Xiang and I weren't really besties (or were we?). And it's not like I even knew Kirby all that well, so I couldn't even really claim him as my friend.

But I couldn't help feeling like I should be more included, you know, like, as some sort of finder's fee?

Then I started wondering whether having a really intense best-friendship with Jimmy had screwed me up. Would I ever be able to have friends like other people and not be all possessive and jealous? It seemed that the only way I knew how to be friends with someone was to completely merge identities.

"You and Kirby were sure chatty this evening," I said, perversely stoking the embers of my annoyance.

"Yeah, he's a funny guy. We were mostly talking about the different guys he's dating online. Seattle's being evasive, so Kirby is starting to write him off. But Omaha forgave him, so he's back to being the favorite."

"Sounds complicated."

"Yeah," she murmured groggily.

"Were you discussing Parker with him?"

"Yeah, a little," she said, then yawned widely. "God, I've become such a horndog. Unlike you, I can't *stop* thinking about my guy. I just wanna lick him aaall over."

"Eww."

Was that how I was supposed to be feeling about Felix right now? I mean, I enjoyed the kiss, but I definitely wasn't wanting to—eww.

I felt queasy, and I don't think it was the beer.

Maybe I was OK with Kirby taking on some areas of Xiang's friendship, after all.

Xiang, meanwhile, was fast asleep.

On Monday morning I got an e-mail from Felix (finally!).

Hey—
Can't wait to see you at rehearsal tomorrow.
F

How cute was that? I could just picture his dimpled smile as he typed it between classes. *sigh* And he sent it from his *personal* e-mail address, not his school one.

:)

Meanwhile, Jenny had e-mailed out the rehearsal schedule, which she had made on a spreadsheet program. She should work for the CIA, because trained code-breakers with PhDs and supercomputers wouldn't be able to make heads or tails of it. OK, maybe it wasn't that bad—and I'm sure it was hard to put together, since we each had our own dates when we couldn't rehearse—but Xiang had to help me for a good ten minutes at lunch before I figured out that I would have only seven rehearsals with Felix.

Yup, you read that right: *seven*.

The first of which was tomorrow. The boys in the cast

had a few separate rehearsal days on weekends, probably because they had to travel more, and a lot of the music rehearsals split the cast into smaller groups to work with Mrs. Murray. Little Red Riding Hood basically only has one musical scene with the Wolf, and not really any with Cinderella's Prince (except for full-cast scenes), so Felix and I were put into separate groups. Most of our "together" rehearsals would be in a few weeks, when we started doing our dress rehearsals.

Aaaaaargh!!!

Xiang was lucky: All her orchestra rehearsals would include Parker, obviously. And it looked like poor Jimmy and Oliver had to be at every rehearsal except the ones that were just about the music. (I couldn't even imagine what horrible tasks Jenny had already begun dreaming up for them . . .) So I supposed *that* was one good thing about the schedule. Last night's bowling with Oliver had been totally fun, and until the performances in mid-November, I'd have lots of time with both of my favorite gay boys.

But very little time with the boy I *most* wanted to have around. (Pout.)

"You know," Xiang said, taking a drag from her cigarette, "you could see him *not* at rehearsal. Then you wouldn't even have to sneak around. And it's not like *your* parents are breathing down your neck, monitoring you all the time."

I kicked absentmindedly at the brick wall behind Jerry Hall. Xiang had started smoking after lunch every day now. She'd found a spot just outside the rear entrance to the theater where no one ever went, and she could pollute her lungs undetected by any teachers.

"I don't think he's gotten his driver's license yet," I said, "even though he is a junior. Maybe he'll get it soon, like Oliver will? That would make everything soooo much simpler."

"Assuming he also gets, or has access to, a car," she reminded me, stubbing what little was left of her cigarette on the cracked concrete walkway.

Curses. "Well, his sister had a car, so maybe it's an extra family car that he could also use?"

Xiang didn't say anything.

For about half a minute, we watched a red-tailed hawk circle high above.

"But you're right," I said, finally breaking the spell. "I'm being a baby. We can totally see each other outside of rehearsal. But, I mean, *I'm* sure as heck not going to ask *him* to hang out. Maybe he'll ask me."

She rolled her eyes. "What's the big deal? *You* be the decider. You've hooked up with the boy, so you should at least be able to speak to him."

"It's not like that—not for us. I get all clumsy and inarticulate around him. I don't even know why. I guess it's 'cause he's older and confident and . . . it can be kinda scary. But also scary in a good way. Know what I mean?"

"No," Xiang said flatly. "But I bet Parker does. He seems a little scared of me, actually."

"Yeah? I can see that."

Xiang narrowed her eyes at me. "Bitch."

* * * * *

At dinner that evening my parents were in rare form. By that I mean, "a form that is not nearly rare enough."

As my mother passed me the marinated-tofu latkes, I sensed an uncomfortable vibe in the air. She kept glancing at my dad, and he was quieter than usual—but not the good kind of silence I would normally consider a blessing.

"Soooo, is anyone going to tell me what's up?" I finally ventured, no longer able to bear the tension.

My mother tucked a stray lock of graying hair behind one ear and moved her pointed stare from my father to me.

"Well, actually, there is something your father and I want to discuss with you." She twirled her fork around, grinding a cylindrical hole into her parsnip-and-apple compote. "We think it's time for us to set some ground rules for you and your friends."

"Ground rules," I repeated, uncomprehending.

"Yes, ground rules. You're no longer a young girl, and the way you socialize with your cohorts is changing. We wouldn't be doing our job as your parents if we didn't respond accordingly."

Oh, God. I knew it would be bad once she started being all clinical about it.

"You're entering an age when your friends may be discovering aspects about their bodies—"

"Eww! Mom!" I barked, my shoulders instinctively seizing up.

"—and we can't just sit idly by while you face all kinds of new social pressures. Isn't that right?" Then she did that thing where she widens her eyes at my father, telling him it's time for him to step in.

My dad cleared his throat. "Yes, that's correct. You're a teenager now, Marty, and we understand that it's not an easy age. You and your friends are growing older, and we know how hard it can be to stay true to your values."

"Honestly, I don't think I'm capable of rolling my eyes hard enough for this. This is exactly like you sending me to Oaks because you think—"

Ignoring me, he continued: "With that in mind, we're going to try our best to create an environment for you that is safe, structured, and as free of those pressures as possible."

"Can we please speak normal English? Whatever this is, it's ridiculous."

"We have never set up clear rules for you before now, because we didn't believe you needed them at your young age. But now that you and your friends are older—"

"Since when are you two so interested in 'my friends'?" I interjected, my exasperated mood starting to tilt toward defensive anger.

"—we need to make them explicit. So here they are." My dad pulled out a Post-it note that he had scrawled all over. I could see that my anger made him angry, and some tiny, wise part of me started warning me to pull back.

As if!

"One. You will be home by ten on school nights, and midnight on Fridays and Saturdays."

"Are you kidding me? You have got to be joking. A curfew? Oh, please! I don't need a curfew."

My mother's eyebrows shot up. "Well, considering the time you came home with Xiang the other night, young lady, I don't think you have much of a leg to stand on."

Damn it, they *had* heard us stumble in. Well, whatever, this was still outrageous.

My father's voice grew louder. "Two. No phone calls longer than ten minutes. Three. We can't monitor what you do online all the time, but we will be keeping an eye on you. Don't ever forget that."

I folded my arms across my chest. "Oh, is that a rule? Great, yeah, that's a good one. I'll be sure to *not ever forget that.*"

"Four. If you do go out, we want to know where you are going, whom you are going with, and for how long," he said. "You don't leave this house without your cell, and you don't turn it off." Then he blushed a little as he added, "And five, if you have male visitors, you keep the door open the entire time."

"*What?*" I was flabbergasted. "Like . . . Jimmy?"

"Well, yeah. Jimmy and his friends. Boys."

"As if . . . me and Jimmy—I mean, seriously? You know he's *gay*, right?"

This time it was my mother who rolled her eyes. "We're not *morons,* Martha."

My father cleared his throat. "From the looks of it, when he and his friends came here the other night, there are romantic interests brewing—"

"*Romantic interests brewing?*" I said/shrieked. "If you want to know, just ASK. Yes, Jimmy and Derek are a couple.

So what? And now it seems you think me and 'my friends' are wild, sex-crazed hooligans."

They just sat there, looking at me impassively, a black thundercloud of tension hovering over the room, crackling with electricity.

"See, this is the part where you say, 'Oh, no, that's not what we think at all. You're totally right: You're good kids! In fact, we're lucky to have such a Goody-Two-Shoes for a daughter, with such upstanding gentlemen for friends! And you know what? Scratch everything we just said. We were just being *jerks.'*"

As soon as I spat out the word—with surprising venom—I realized it was a strategic blunder. They were clearly taken aback. I knew I was only confirming their unhinged fears that I was turning into a Bad Kid. But I was so mad at that point, I was so incensed, I couldn't go back. And the only way forward was up a notch.

"Like, my friends are going to come over here to *screw*? *Really?*" I was dizzy with rage.

"This has nothing to do—" my mother began, but I would not be derailed.

"You know what?" I leaned forward on trembling hands. "*I hate you.*"

On that charming note, I got up from the table and flew upstairs to my room, slamming the door so hard that my ears hummed for a good five seconds afterward.

Oh, well, so much for dinner. I lay down on my bed, staring holes into the ceiling and replaying the blowup in my mind. I came up with about twenty better rejoinders that I wish I had said (and thrown my food! and knocked over my chair!) before my blood pressure started easing off.

I tossed and turned, then jumped up and paced the room, then grew tired and returned to the bed.

Breathe in, breathe out.

Breathe in, breathe out.

Eventually the anger started to subside, displaced by a heavy sadness that lay over me. I knew that even if this disastrous dinner could someday be smoothed over and forgotten, it would never be the same with my parents. This was just one more nail in the coffin around our relationship, a coffin they had started building by sending me to Our Lady of the Oaks. I'm a *person*. I have feelings and opinions and rights. But they just didn't give a shit.

When I thought about how it was just one year ago, I could remember joking around with my parents like we were buddies, and I'd felt closer to them than any of my friends were to their parents. They were often lame and embarrassing, sure, but they could be fun! They liked me, and I liked them!

But now, more and more they were aspiring to be some kind of weird, enemy authority figures. Did they really want to be like Xiang's parents? They thought I was changing—and maybe I was—but to my mind, they were the ones who were changing, for the worse.

The stereotype of a teenage girl, sullen and withdrawn, was something that had always seemed foreign and counterintuitive to me. But suddenly it seemed to be the only available option. The only leverage I had with my parents was myself, and that's something they wouldn't get to access anymore. They want to create rules and put up barriers? Fine. But I can build barriers, too.

Jerks.

But perhaps there was one tiny sliver of a silver lining in this shitstorm: This definitely called for a foray into my secret Twix stash. I grabbed one bar (OK, two) and flopped back onto my bed.

For a second, I considered running away. No, not like to New York or something—don't be ridiculous—just slipping out of the house, heading through the woods, and crashing with Jimmy. But what would that solve, really? Nothing.

More to the point, this was one fight that I didn't want to talk over with Jimmy; I mean, I didn't want him to feel weird around my parents. They'd known him forever, and now all of sudden they apparently saw him as some sort of sex fiend.

Plus, it was raining.

I fingered my phone. I wanted to call Oliver, but that would have been weird, right? I really didn't know him *that* well, to call up and complain about my parents.

Instead, I texted Xiang.

my parents r evil – ive SO joind yr club :(

I couldn't wait to see Felix the next day. Mom and Dad think I'm bad? Oh, I can be bad.

I can be *very* bad.

ou need to *relax*," urged Xiang. We were walking to the rehearsal room from her locker, and she was lagging far behind.

Poor Xiang. From the moment I laid eyes on her in Mr. Dartagnan's class, all throughout lunch, and in four long diatribes/e-mails sent between classes, I'd vented my anger about my parents. She was trying to be sympathetic, but since her own parents were even more crazy-strict, it was clearly a strain.

"I'm relaxed! I'm totally relaxed. Who isn't relaxed?" I muttered, yanking open the entrance doors to Jerry Hall. I stalked through the lobby, pushed open the auditorium doors, and ran into Jenny McCafferty.

Like, literally rammed my forehead into her skull. Bangs to headband. There was a hollow knocking sound and a flash of white as I sank to my knees, but I managed not to pass out. I smiled stupidly at this accomplishment.

Jenny, on the other hand, chose to go with a different reaction: red-hot fury. "WHAT THE HELL?" she spat, rubbing her head and glaring at me.

Oliver had been following right behind her, and he dropped his clipboard and script to rush to my side.

"Oh, my God, Marty, are you OK? Does it hurt?" he asked, his big brown eyes floating in front of me, full of concern.

"Yeah, I'm fine," I said, wincing. "Just embarrassed, I guess."

"WHAT THE HELL?" Jenny repeated, red-faced, although this time directing her rage at Oliver.

He cast her a sidelong glance. "Oh, Jenny. Sorry. You OK?"

She huffed indignantly, then turned and marched out into the lobby.

"I think that means she's fine," he said, gathering his things and standing. He offered his hand and lifted me up. He leaned in close. "Hey, if you feel like you want to fall asleep, don't."

Then he was off, ducking into the lobby—just as Xiang finally caught up.

"Jesus, you're fast," she heaved. "What's with the noggin?"

"Noggin?" I asked.

"Yeah, your forehead is all red."

Shit. Shit, shit, shit.

Xiang pushed me toward the girls' bathroom. "I can't take you anywhere, can I? Look, I'll do what I can, but I gotta get going soon to *my* rehearsal."

Five minutes later, with my bangs awkwardly plastered in vain over a sizeable bump, I was sitting in Rehearsal Room B as Sister Mary Alice talked us through the set design and what it would mean for how we moved around onstage. I tried to hold my script out in a way that blocked Felix's view of me.

Typical. The plan for today was to take my flirtation with Felix to the next level, not have him confuse me with the Elephant Man!

Felix was wearing his St. Paul's uniform, and his slim physique was perfectly served by his fitted charcoal pants and dress shirt. (He had taken off his tie, of course.) I mean, I don't know what hair products that boy uses, but his dark locks are perpetually shiny without looking oily, and they're wavy in a classic way that makes me think of ancient Greek sculptures.

We started blocking the first act, so I had a bunch of time to kill at the back of the room with Jimmy, Derek, and Oliver, pretending to memorize lyrics. I figured that as long as I stayed with them, Felix would probably keep a safe distance from my forehead. Then, when I had to go up and run through my scene, Sister Mary Alice was either too blind or too gracious to comment on my new head tumor, but I was convinced everyone else was staring at it. (Everyone except Jenny, who pointedly refused to look at me.) I managed to get through the act, and when Sister announced a break, I rushed into the girls' bathroom. I needed to see what my second head had started to look like by this point.

As I hovered over the sink, trying out different angles to see if I could find one that didn't scream, "Freakish! Misshapen!," someone said, "You know you're the only one who sees anything there, right?"

The voice belonged to Kate O'Day. Remember her? She's Cinderella, the beautiful senior who sang "Popular" at the auditions. I had pretty much steered clear of her up to this point, so this was the first time she had ever spoken to me (excluding times like games of Freeze at auditions, but social rules don't apply when you're acting). She stood at the sink next to me, both of her hands flicking pointlessly at her thick auburn hair, as if it weren't already perfectly arranged.

"Yeah, well," I said lamely, not sure how to answer.

She sighed and said, "I'm so glad we're doing *Into the Woods*. And I think we have a pretty great cast this year, don't you? Like, better than normal."

"Yeah," I said, nodding my head like a bobblehead doll.

She caught my eye in the mirror and broke into a sheepish grin. "You're a first-year, aren't you? So you wouldn't even know." I stopped nodding. "But, anyway, trust me, this cast is way better than last year's."

She was being kinda nice and really patronizing at the same time. It was very confusing.

"I mean, think about it. There's Maria, who is amazing, right? I wish I could sing like her. And you're really good. And Felix—I mean, he has to come all the way down from St. Paul's to get here, so we're really lucky to have him in the show."

"Oh, he does?" I said, trying to make it seem like I hadn't really given Felix much thought.

She nodded. Then her eyes, pale blue like sea glass, rose to refocus on my forehead.

"Honestly, I can't see a thing." With that, she turned and sauntered out of the bathroom.

I went back into the rehearsal room in a fog. Jenny was talking animatedly to Jimmy and Oliver in a corner. Oliver said something, and the others cracked up, Jenny's whole body heaving in exaggerated spasms. God, she was annoying.

Oliver caught my eye and gave me a chin-lift acknowledgment, so I reluctantly started to make my way over. I mean, I wanted to hang out with him but not her.

And then Felix stepped into my path.

"Hey, you."

I stopped, very close to him, and instinctively adopted a coy slouch, meeting his eyes with a sideways smile. Where on earth had I ever learned these things?

"Hey," I said.

"You were really good earlier," he said slowly, his dimples appearing and disappearing in rhythm as he spoke. My mind raced: "earlier"? *The kiss from last week?*

Oh, he must mean earlier in the rehearsal. My hand instinctively flew up to my forehead to pull at my bangs and hide my probably gargantuan bruise.

"You weren't so bad yourself," I said, wondering if I was smiling too hard, like a baboon baring its gums.

Then there was this weird moment when Felix and I just stared at each other. It was almost like déjà vu or something, since it felt a lot like . . . remembering? I know this makes zero sense, but it's as if I was recognizing Felix from some time before, that we really *knew* each other. I mean, I look into people's eyes in conversation all the time, but with him it just felt incredibly intimate. My face grew hot.

"I mean," I sputtered, "you must have been acting for a long time."

"Yeah, I love doing this," he said. "Even though we have all these lines to say and places to stand and timing to follow, for some reason it's incredibly freeing. Liberating. Y'know?" I nodded eagerly, but he looked down, suddenly bashful. "I don't know what I'm saying," he said. "I probably sound crazy."

"No, not at all," I replied quickly, thinking about how our earlier discussion of his craziness had led to . . . kissing. And suddenly we were looking into each other's eyes again. How can something so simple and commonplace as *looking* suddenly be so amazing?

Then the spell was broken by Sister Mary Alice clapping her hands to quiet the room down. "Let's get back to business," she said.

"Anyway," Felix said, "I'll see you around." He gave me a two-fingered salute—a metaphorical tipping of the hat—and walked over to where he had left off blocking before the break. I sank into a nearby seat, smiling stupidly.

Suddenly I felt a pressure on top of my head. It took a second to realize that it was two hands, gently resting there. I leaned my head back to see Oliver's face above me, upside down. His eyes were closed, and he was softly humming a single, sustained note.

"Um, are you having a stroke?" I whispered.

"Au contraire," he said quietly, eyes still closed. "I'm healing you."

Oh, Oliver. What a cutie. "What, no kiss to make it better?" I teased.

"When duty calls," he said and then laid a soft kiss upon my forehead.

"Much better," I said. "I think I might just pull through and live to see another day."

"You'd better," he said. "I'm not sure I'd be a particularly good Little Red Riding Hood stand-in. That, uh, Wolf scene would take on a whole new angle, wouldn't it?"

"Now, *that* I would like to see," I said, giggling. "You and Felix would make such a cute coup—"

But before I could finish, Jenny suddenly appeared and hissed at me, "Marty, you really need to keep it down. Some of us are taking this rehearsal kind of seriously."

My ears flamed hot with shame, and she snapped at Oliver, "I need you in the other room."

Oliver, mugging a terrified expression, trailed after her.

Whatever. I sat back and contented myself with watching Felix. He was working on the scene with Sister Mary Alice and Kate O'Day in which the Prince discovers Cinderella. With his classic smile and baritone intonation, he was doing a great job—I mean, who could ever resist him?

But after a few minutes of watching Felix act and interact with Kate, my forehead bruise started to pulse with a dull pain, then edge toward a full-fledged headache.

Stupid crash with Jenny.

Felix tucked a lock of hair behind his ear, and it struck me that, *actually*, his ears are kind of weird; they stick out. His mop of wavy hair totally hides them.

No disproportional ears on stunning Kate.

Felix fumbled a line, and Kate laughed loudly. No honking horse laughs with that girl, either; this was a melodious, lilting, *pretty* laugh. The mistake wasn't even that funny, but she sure was giggly around Felix. And she had just told me five minutes before that she thought we were lucky to have him around . . .

I stared hard at him. Was he acting, or was he *really* hitting on her? I shook my head and took a deep breath. As funky as I was feeling, I knew I was being nutso. I mean, it sounds really cheesy, but Felix and I really were, like, love at first sight. Instant chemistry.

I wondered what Xiang's reaction to Parker was the first time they met. Was that how it normally happened for everyone? One day you meet, and—BAM!—two magnets slamming against each other?

Jimmy rolled his eyes at me as he hustled by, carefully balancing a dusty stack of colored gels for the spotlights. *His* connection with Derek had been pretty immediate.

I turned to watch Derek pacing by himself in the back, muttering, trying to memorize lines. I don't think he realized that the lyrics would be a million times easier to remember when set to music; we'd start singing everything at Thursday's first music-only rehearsal with Mrs. Murray.

Derek should at least be listening to the sound track on his phone. He was so nervous, though, I figured I'd leave him be. Where nerves are concerned, whatever helps.

Then I looked back at Felix and Kate working on their scene with Sister. Felix caught my eye and broke into a grin.

A genuine *"Man, it's great to know you"* grin.

I scrunched my nose in smiling acknowledgment.

I had nothing to worry about.

After rehearsal, as everyone dispersed, I walked reluctantly toward my dad's car. I still hadn't spoken a word to either of my parents since last night. They, in turn, had regarded me frostily, like I should be apologizing to them for something.

As if.

"How was rehearsal?" asked Dad as I climbed in.

"Fine," I replied tersely, staring out the window.

He sighed heavily, and we didn't speak another word the whole way home.

The next morning I was drinking from the water fountain when I felt someone sidle up next to me. I assumed it was Xiang, so I snorted some water up my nose when I turned to see Maria Kilkenny instead, beaming at me.

"Oh, gosh!" she said, suddenly concerned over my coughing up water. "I'm so sorry! I didn't mean to startle you. Sorry."

I managed to recover a bit and gave her a reassuring smile. "No worries."

"I just wanted to say I'm really glad you're in the play. Do you realize we're the only two first-years? I mean, I guess a couple of the guys might be our age."

I hadn't really thought about the fact that she was a freshman before. The Witch was a pretty big role, but, then again, as Kate had pointed out, Maria *was* amazingly talented. It was sobering to think we'd be competitors throughout my whole high school drama career. Good thing we looked so different—me being scrawny and blond, and her being way bigger with dark hair.

And, I reminded myself, it is a lot more fun acting with people who are really good at it.

"Huh," I said, trying to match the brightness of her expression. "I guess we've got to stick together. Defend first-year honor."

"You don't think they'll do some kind of hazing thing to us, do you?" she asked, giggling. "You know, make us do shots and then have us perform 'Tomorrow' or 'Memory' or something?" We started walking down the hall together.

I laughed. "God, I hope so! That would actually be pretty hilarious."

"It would be, wouldn't it . . . ?" She grabbed my arm. "Let's do it, anyway!" Her eyes flashed, and I couldn't help but shrink back from the intensity of her excitement.

Then, just as suddenly, she waved a perfunctory air kiss with one hand and turned into Mr. Livingstone's room, all the while humming the first bars of "Tomorrow."

Maria Kilkenny = lots of fun, apparently?

In Mrs. Mason's English class, while we were supposed to be doing some "quiet reading," I got a text from an unknown number.

Hey, Red, what's shakin?

Ooooh, Felix!

Thank God for having a last name that starts with *S*: I'm pretty much always in the back of the classroom. I propped my book up as a barrier and started typing on the phone.

Not much. Sitting in class, thinkin bout you.

A long moment passed before I got the reply.

Uh . . . really? Did you JUST talk to Jimmy?

Oh, shit. Wait. Was this not Felix?

Sorry, who is this?

An extremely flattered Oliver. Got your number from Jimmy, like, seconds ago.

Suddenly the name "Red" was more appropriate than Oliver could have known, considering how my face looked.

OH! Ha, how funny. Sorry, thought you were someone else.

A second later, I also sent:

A friend.

And a second after that:

Her dog is sick.

Aww, man. That sucks. Sorry.

Oh, no worries. I'm sure it'll be fine.

Could I please stop digging this hole? I'm the worst secret-keeper ever. I kept typing.

So what's up?

Happy Sukkot! It starts Monday.

Huh? I typed:

??? You gonna make me look that up?

Tsk-tsk. What do they teach in those Catholic schools? Sukkot, the joyous Jewish festival of booths!

Oliver was Jewish?

How does your family celebrate?

Er, we're not Jewish. I just like any reason for rejoicing.

Oliver. He's so weird. (In a good way.)

You're so random. But a bit early for Monday, no? Won't I see you in an hour?

Nope. Music-only rehearsal, so Jimmy and I are off the hook. And this weekend I'll be fishing in PA with Dad.

Rats. So, happy Sukkot? I guess I'll see you next Tues.

There was a short pause before I got the next text.

Yeah, C U next—WAIT, DID YOU JUST SWEAR AT ME?

I laughed out loud but then tried to hide it in a coughing fit when Mrs. Mason looked over at me.

"Martha," she said sternly. "Time to focus."

"Myyyy mother makes me mash my M&MMMMMMs!"

The whole cast belted scales, hitting the high note on "mash" before plummeting down to the low note again. Mrs. Murray overemphasized each word, her mouth expanding to a great maw and then contracting to a pinch. She must make it really easy for her dentist, I thought as I painfully stretched my own lips as wide as they would go.

"Again!" she shouted, holding up a clenched fist as if she were Evita Perón on the balcony of the Casa Rosada. (If you don't know, go watch the movie. Madonna!)

"Myyyy mother makes me . . ."

Oh, good Lord. Even higher?

"Myyyy mother makes me . . ."

Higher, really?

Warm-up vocal exercises were a lot more intense than I'd ever had in middle-school theater, that's for sure. Maybe *this* was the hazing Maria had joked about?

On the other hand, it felt good to finally apply myself to something, to pull out the stops and really see if I could cut it. I saw beads of sweat forming on Derek's forehead as he strained to hit the high note, but he did hit it, impressively.

Felix, on the other hand, had long since given up, smiling duck-lips (still cute!) and shaking his head in disbelief and admiration at everyone still in the running. Maria, of course, was totally killing it, her operatic soprano notes filling the room. I hated-slash-loved her.

Music rehearsals felt totally different from the other rehearsals, where we were scattered about and working on various things, like some chaotic insect colony slowly working toward a single goal in a thousand different ways. Here, however, we were a single organism, with Mrs. Murray as the brain; I mean, she really embraced "director" in the title "music director." We were like the pipes of a church organ, arrayed before her and responding to her lightning-quick pointing.

"Now you, Cinderella! Jason! Penelope, louder!"

If you've ever heard *Into the Woods*, you'll know that it's way complicated; unlike most musicals, it doesn't have people singing their own songs and then joining together for a duet or an ensemble piece every once in a while. This show has those traditional songs, sure, but a lot of the show is basically conversations set to music—conversations with ten people involved. People are constantly interjecting little phrases, explaining things, weaving different sentences together—it's a nightmare for performers, basically. If anyone misses a line, it throws the whole thing off. Christy is a super-impressive piano player, but she basically only kept time and played the top notes that we would be singing, no chords or intros or interludes or anything.

At first, a lot of people were worried about how some of the songs didn't seem to have a melody.

"It's just words and notes," Derek complained. "They don't . . . go together."

But the more you listen to it, the more you can hear the melody. And, in fact, soon you can't get the melody out of your head. Eventually it becomes a part of you; it becomes so perfect in your mind that you can't imagine the song going any other way.

"*. . . into the woods to Grandmother's house and home before dark!*"

When we were sitting in the rehearsal room, I started to get a much better sense of how people were going to perform onstage. When Maria rapped her song about losing her magical beans, she wasn't afraid to ham it up. This meant that whenever she *really* sang, it came as an even more impressive revelation. She was so good, she didn't have to show it all the time. It's funny how confidence works in different ways in theater: It's not just about putting your insecurities aside; it's about putting your pride aside, too.

"Martha. Martha! You missed it." Mrs. Murray waved at Christy to stop. I frantically glanced down. Oh, shit. My cue. But which one?

"I—"

"You jump in on *See it's your fault!*" Mrs. Murray said. "Let's take it again. One, two, three . . ."

I flushed crimson, embarrassed. Here I was, evaluating everyone else, thinking I had this all down. This was going to take a lot more concentration, clearly.

Felix wasn't helping the situation, of course. It seemed that every time I looked up, he was looking at me.

And I looked up a lot.

At Tuesday's rehearsal Oliver had a present for me. Derek was up onstage pretending to feed a cow, Jimmy was going over sound cues with Jenny, and Felix had gone outside for a phone call. I was sitting on the floor in a corner, trying to get through my algebra problem set, when Oliver walked over and slumped down next to me.

"Howdy," he said.

"Well, well. If it isn't Mr. Sukkot. Am I pronouncing that right?"

"Uh . . . no idea. Let's just say yes?"

"How was the fishing expedition?

Oliver sighed heavily. "Horrible. As expected."

"Really?"

"I can't stand fishing. It's so painfully boring. The worst. But my dad gets worried about me not being butch enough."

"Aww, I think you're plenty butch."

He grinned. "Why, thank you. I appreciate that." He reached into his pocket. "It's ridiculous that my dad worries about it, and it's not like he himself doesn't realize that it's ridiculous, but . . . well, it is what it is. So I humor him. And, bonus! I brought you a souvenir."

He held out a fist and dropped a pebble into my out-stretched palm.

"Wow. Some girls obsess about getting a rock someday." The pebble was gray and smooth; I rubbed it with my fingers, luxuriating in its surprising silkiness.

"It's precious," Oliver said. "It was spared being skipped, unlike four thousand of its riverbed-mates. Take good care of it."

Jenny suddenly materialized above us. "Martha, it's your turn out in the hall."

Man! If she wasn't pulling Oliver away for something, she was sending me somewhere else. She turned and marched away, her clipboard clutched to her chest and her shoulders seesawing with every step. I wrenched my own shoulders back and forth, a busybody imitation that bumped against Oliver.

He bumped me back before I managed to struggle up to a standing position.

This week each of the cast members had to get measured for our costumes. One at a time, Jenny was sending us out into the hall, where Calliope Connor was busy working a tape measure.

Now, Calliope was the perfect choice for the role of costume designer. She was constantly being called in for "discussions" with Sister Margaret, the vice principal, because of her crazy hair extensions and the different ways she hacked our uniform. For Calliope, dressing for school every day seemed to be some kind of *Project Runway* challenge.

"Sister, I read the policy very carefully," she'd say sweetly. "I didn't see any rule against adding shoulder pads. They're excellent padding for these heavy book-bag straps!" Or, from the look of them, excellent for an NFL game or a Tartar invasion.

Naturally, she was taking our costumes very seriously.

In the corridor, Calliope had arrayed all her fabric samples, shoes of different sizes, and tangled piles of measuring tape in haphazard rows. She got straight to work, measuring my arms and my bust—however lacking it is—and taking careful notes.

"Do you need to turn your head a lot onstage?" she asked, reviewing a questionnaire she had written up.

"Uh, yeah. I think so," I said, thrown by the question.

"Oh, that's too bad," she said, frowning hard. "Hmm."

Oh, dear. What was she planning?

"And the red cape. Do you have to wear it the whole time?"

"No, it definitely has to come off. The Baker takes it from me, in fact. And it gets fed to the cow."

Calliope looked disappointed again, and she scratched several lines off her list of questions. "I'm having trouble figuring you out," she said, shaking her head. "How old are you?"

"Um, fourteen. Fifteen in December."

She glanced up at me, and it was clear from her face that she thought I was the dumbest person on the planet.

"Oh—you mean my character!" I exclaimed, fully mortified. "Ha-ha. Um, you know, just generally a kid? Old enough to go into the woods by myself but young enough to be really scared?"

That made her laugh. "That doesn't narrow it down much, now does it?"

But let's not forget about Felix.

How could I?

Unfortunately, sneaking around with him was a lot harder than I had imagined. During the entire month of October, we only managed to find *a few* more chances to duck into an empty room (or, on one occasion, the janitor's closet) to kiss some more. We didn't even really talk to each other; we'd make eye contact, he'd tilt his head toward some room, and then we'd drift away from everyone else—separately—find each other in there, and, well, make out. All tongues and hot breath. But we didn't dare stay long, so, like, thirty seconds later we'd duck back out, one at a time, and act as if nothing had happened.

These moments weren't all that much (or many) in terms of making-out action, but they made being at rehearsals excruciatingly . . . *electric*. We had this massive secret, this crazy attraction, and it took all our acting abilities to keep it natural and cool. During breaks we'd gravitate toward each other—totally unplanned, I swear—so we'd both end up standing by the entrance lobby, or the stairwell to the dressing rooms, or the snack machine. But there were other people around, too, of course, so I don't think anyone noticed anything odd about it. We were just hyperaware of each other, all the time.

Occasionally his hand would brush past mine, and a tingling sensation would blossom over the rest of me.

My lips ached.

So, to make a long story short(er), that's basically the situation that continued all throughout the whole month of October. Xiang kept getting *closer* with Parker—and telling Kirby all about it, not me. Jimmy and I weren't spending as much time together as we'd hoped: At rehearsals he was always running around doing Jenny McCafferty's bidding, and otherwise he was disappearing without a trace into Derek World.

But, honestly, I didn't mind too much. I was busy doing insane amounts of homework (child-labor-law violations!), going to endless rehearsals, smooching Felix in a dark corner every once in a blue moon, and getting my snark on with Xiang and Oliver. In fact, Oliver and I got into the habit of sending funny texts to each other pretty much every day.

And I said about three words to my parents the whole time.

In the middle of the month was Set Day, when the whole cast was required to come in on a Saturday to help construct the set. We were really excited and energetic for the first few hours in the morning, when the sketches were passed around and the power tools came out. Then the pizzas arrived for lunch. But when the afternoon wore on, and the monotony of painting leaves or hammering various rolling walls together set in, it became . . . a drag. A boring, annoying drag.

Jenny's bossiness didn't help matters. On the other hand, I was getting pretty good at imitating her dorky mannerisms. This made me quite popular with the cast, and I kept getting asked to do impromptu performances; Chloe nearly choked to death on her pizza from laughing. (Doing impersonations is a necessary skill for any aspiring actor. Think about it: That's the best part of late-night talk shows, seeing celebrities mock one another!)

At one point, though, Jenny walked in on me mid-impression. Felix tried to warn me, widening his eyes and jerking his head, but I was too absorbed in marking off my "checklist" that I didn't even notice. When I looked up, Jenny was staring—no, glaring—at me. Then she just kind of shook her head and walked out.

Felix burst out laughing, but somehow it didn't seem all that funny anymore.

Actually, it was pretty bad.

But whatever: Had she been acting less irritating, there would have been nothing to mock.

OK, *yes*, it was still bad. And, to be fair, Jenny wasn't the only one being annoying that day. In the morning, while we tried to paint a stone-wall pattern on one of the flats (framed muslin panels that are used as walls onstage), Jimmy kept going on and on about how *hard* it was that Derek didn't go to his school, that Derek lived in Weeksburg, a *twenty-*

minute drive from Bracksville. He made it sound like they lived on different continents and that they never, ever, ever saw each other in this long-distance relationship.

Finally, I couldn't take it anymore. I was, like, "Jimmy. Look around you. No one here lives in the same town as their boyfriend. Think of Xiang. And—hello—Kirby and his many boyfriends? And think of me and *you know.*" I nodded toward Felix, who was trying to screw rolling casters onto the hooves of a giant plastic cow.

That shut Jimmy up, but I could tell he was annoyed that I didn't feel sorry for him. Then my phone buzzed, and I looked at it. The message said, *This is your fault. To think I could be fishing.*

I giggled and looked toward the back of the room, where a bunch of people were tying branches onto a rolling ladder, to serve as Cinderella's wishing tree.

"Who's that from?" asked Jimmy.

"Oh, Oliver," I said.

Jimmy nodded, but he didn't seem too happy about that, either.

Anyway, near the end of the day, I was busy trying to finish applying plastic ivy to the palace wall with a staple gun when Maria Kilkenny tapped me on the shoulder.

"I've been sent on a very important recon mission."

"Oh-ho?" I asked, happy to take a break.

"Yes. It's very, very important," she said solemnly. "Madison thinks"—she nodded her head across the room toward Cinderella's Stepmother—"that Oliver is, in her words, 'way hot.' She also seems to think we're in third grade, which is why she sent me over here."

"I see," I said.

"So. As his friend. Can you confirm or deny that he has a girlfriend?"

Even from fifty feet away, I could see Madison watching us with a crazed, eager look on her face.

"Why, yes, I can definitely deny the existence of any girl-friend."

Maria clapped happily.

"But," I continued, "unfortunately for Madison, Oliver is not looking for a girlfriend."

The clapping froze. "No? Oh, crap, you two aren't going out, are you?"

I snorted in response. "No, it's not like that! He's not looking for any girl. He's crushing on some guy."

Oops. The crush was supposed to be a secret, wasn't it? Oh, well, it had been weeks, and there's gotta be an expira-tion date on secrecy sometime . . .

"Womp-womp," she said, slumping into a slouch. "Just when you think you've found a unicorn in the thea-tahh . . ." Then she shrugged and made her way back to Madison.

When I turned my attention back to my plastic ivy, I heard a "psst" and looked up to see Felix off to the side, beckoning me.

I immediately dropped the staple gun to the floor and nearly pranced over to him, behind some painted flats that were propped up to dry. (Well, what can I say? The days of coy restraint were gone, apparently.) The flats formed a tiny room right in the middle of Set Day activities, and I was pleasantly surprised to find that they completely blocked off the view from everyone else.

"Why, hello," I said quietly, resting a hand on his shoulder.

"Hi, there," he said, his voice deep and low, and he pulled me toward him, drawing me into a kiss. His bottom lip dragged against my bottom lip, and I found myself breathing "Ohhhhh" into his mouth. I mean, I'm sure I had pizza breath, but he didn't seem to notice; he just kept kissing, his tongue licking the edges of my lips.

Suddenly I felt his hand move against my stomach. Like, *under my T-shirt.* I was so startled, I jumped back with an audible "Ah!"

He cringed and looked about wildly, waving to shush me. We stood there, frozen, waiting to hear if anyone had noticed my little outburst.

The coast seemed to be clear. I twisted around to check myself, to be sure I hadn't backed into the wet paint. Seemed OK.

"Sorry," I whispered. "I just didn't—"

"It's fine," he replied softly, pulling me back into his embrace.

"I don't think I'm quite . . . I mean, not yet," I said lamely. I rested my cheek against his shoulder, and he stroked my hair for a moment.

Suddenly I heard a girl's voice call out, "Felix? Is Felix here?"

Whoever she was, she sounded annoyed.

Felix's whole body clenched up. I looked up at his face, which was contorted into a grimace of pain. "Fuck," he whispered. "My sister."

Then he perfunctorily pulled away from me and ducked out of our little room.

"Jill! Relax," I heard him say.

"*There* you are!" she exclaimed. "I've been waiting for forty-five minutes! You said to come pick you up at five . . ." I listened to their voices recede before emerging from the secret room.

As far as I could tell, no one in the room had noticed a thing.

That was a close one.

ooth decay?" Jimmy asked, incredulous. "You're dressed as *tooth decay*?"

Halloween was on a Saturday this year, and Derek, Kirby, and I had come to Jimmy's house to hand out candy while his parents went to some concert in the city. Jimmy's dad had bought a whole bunch of Butterfingers but nothing else, so Jimmy had the brilliant idea to pay his little sister, Jeanie, to collect better candy for us from all the other houses on the street.

But with Jeanie's outfit, it wasn't looking very promising. Her body was covered in rumpled brown paper bags, and her face and hair were smeared with red and brown paint. The words TOOTH DECAY were scrawled across her front in white.

"Yes," she sniffed. "Kids should know what they're getting themselves into. Knowledge is power."

Derek gave her a reassuring smile. "That's very sensible!"

Jeanie rewarded him with a rare smile.

"This is hopeless," Jimmy said, defeated. "Go. Just go. See what you can get."

But Jeanie stayed standing in the foyer, looking at him expectantly.

Exasperated, he dug into his pocket and pulled out a five-dollar bill. *"Go."*

She grabbed the bill, shoved it under her paper shell, and turned to leave.

"Hold up!" Jimmy suddenly called out.

"What?" Jeanie huffed.

"Who are you going with?"

"Penny and her dad."

Jimmy looked at his sister suspiciously. I could tell he was trying to decide whether "Penny" even existed. But then the doorbell rang.

"That's them," she said, and she disappeared out the front door.

Jimmy got up to look out the window to confirm her story.

"I don't mean to be harsh, but that is one wacked-out little girl," Kirby said, shaking his head.

"You don't know the half of it," Jimmy mumbled. "And I could've just *bought* better candy with that money." He was apparently satisfied with what he saw, because he lumbered back to the couch and sank down next to Derek.

This was my first-ever Halloween as a high school student, which seemed to mean no more dressing up. I was a bit depressed about that, I have to say.

The doorbell rang again, and we all four looked at one another. "So, who's gonna get it?" asked Jimmy.

Tick.

Tock.

Eventually, I rolled my eyes, got up from the couch, and

walked to the front door. Through the glass I saw a very handsome cowboy standing under the porch light.

"Howdy, ma'am," Oliver said from under his hat when I opened the door.

"Well, well!" I exclaimed. "To quote one of the girls in the show, you look 'way hot.'"

"Nice! I'm developing a following, then?" he asked, grinning.

Then his face fell when he realized I wasn't in costume. He bounded past me toward the living room, his cowboy boots clicking against the foyer's tile floor. He stared at Kirby, Derek, and Jimmy.

"What? Y'all aren't dressed up? It's Halloween!"

Kirby shook his head. "It's pointless, man. They only give candy to kids. We're too old."

"But that's not the point!" Oliver said. "It's a joyous holiday!"

"Any reason to rejoice, huh?" I said, giving him a knowing look.

He grinned at me, the happiest-looking cowboy I'd ever seen. "Absolutely right."

"Uh, what?" asked Jimmy.

"Oh, it's—never mind," I said. "Not worth explaining."

"It involves booths," said Oliver unhelpfully.

Kirby took in Oliver's getup. "So, tonight, are you going for a *Brokeback Mountain* kind of thing?"

Oliver looked down at his black leather vest, bandana, and faded jeans. "I just threw this together at home. But I think some elements may, in fact, be part of a Village People outfit."

"*Anyway,*" I said, trying to steer the conversation away from Gay Things, "what's the actual plan for tonight?"

"Well," said Jimmy, switching to his business mode, "we've got some board games in the other room. Or movies. Or video games. Or just food."

"Maybe board games are best, since the doorbell will be ringing every few seconds?" said Derek.

"Excellent point!" Jimmy gave Derek a peck on the cheek before going to retrieve the games.

"Where's Xiang?" asked Oliver.

I was about to answer when Kirby said, "She's out with Parker, if you can believe it."

Well, *he* certainly seemed to be updated.

"But if anybody asks," he continued, "she was at Marty's the whole time." Kirby winked broadly.

"How do you *do* that?" asked Derek, amazed. "I'm not a good winker. I can't wink."

We all tried to wink as slowly as possible. It reminded me of that early lunch with Xiang, when we'd tested our stiff upper lips. I realized I missed her, which I figured to be a good thing: It was a sign that we really were a group.

Then I found myself wondering: How would Felix fit in?

It wasn't long before Jeanie came back, way early and with a surprisingly large haul. ("Penny got a little scared by something I did" was all she said by way of explanation.) So we gorged ourselves on sugar until we practically hallucinated. Seeing little kids in Spider-Man and *Frozen* outfits every few minutes only added to the surrealism of the evening. To top it off, we chose to play Risk, which, if you don't already know, is a terrible, horrible game. It was all kinds of nightmarish. I don't want to get into the details of what happened, but the game takes forever, it's too complicated, people drop out too fast (OK, *I* drop out too fast), and by the end people get downright nasty. Jimmy's a really bad loser, too, so after Oliver knocked him out of the game, Jimmy went off to sulk in the kitchen. Which, of course, meant that Derek basically committed imperial suicide in order to leave the game, too. Kirby ended up winning, but he had to totally backstab Oliver to do it.

Never play Risk.

Never.

Monday featured a long, tiring night at rehearsal (sans Felix). Memorizing, blocking, stopping and starting, turning this way, walking that way, trying to squeeze in some algebra backstage . . . This play was a marathon.

Jimmy called my cell just as I was getting into bed. And getting into bed was trickier than it sounds: My room had slowly devolved into a major disaster zone since rehearsals had started, with clothes and notebooks piled up everywhere. When would I ever have time to clean?

"My quirky collard green!"

"More like your sleepy celery stalk at the moment," I replied, tossing some folders to the floor and trying to bury myself under the covers so my evil parents couldn't tell I was on the phone so late at night. (They were clearly into rule-setting, having limited the *duration* of any calls, so there was no need to point out other potential areas for their involvement.)

"Oh, pish," Jimmy chided me. "Sleep when you're dead. We barely got to talk today, and you're the whole reason I'm hauling ass down to your school every other day."

"I thought *Derek* was the whole reason you were there," I mumbled. I felt something poking into my side, and I realized I still had my keys in the pocket of my jeans, and I was lying on them.

"Aww, Derek. He's so stressed about this whole thing," Jimmy whined, not even bothering to address my accusation. "He never imagined he'd get a part, and then he felt like he couldn't turn it down, and now he's just a mess. Poor thing."

"Yeah, well." I yawned audibly. Rehearsals were exhausting, all my unfinished homework was exhausting, and Jimmy's yammering on about Derek was exhausting. I fished out the keys and clicked the mini-flashlight on the key chain. On, off. On, off.

"I mean, it's pretty bad now—how do you think he'll be when it's for real? I mean, it's so bizarre that someone can be so *good* at something and yet not like doing it."

"Hmm." On, off.

"But I think he secretly *does* enjoy it. Deep down. I can tell."

At the moment, I could not care less about Derek and his problems. On, off. Then—*click*—the flashlight didn't turn on. *Click. Click. Click.* Nothing. The battery must have died.

Jimmy kept on. "But he is really good, isn't he? I didn't even know he could sing before he opened his mouth at the audition! I wish he'd just be able to see how good he is, and then he wouldn't be so nervous anymore. Don't you think?"

I couldn't help but remember how Jimmy used to gush about how good of a singer *I* was. I peeked out from under the covers and tossed the keys over to my book bag.

"Jimmy," I said, "I gotta go to sleep."

There was a long pause.

For once, I didn't know what Jimmy was thinking.

"OK. Yeah, you should get to bed," he finally said.

"Jimmy—"

But he had already hung up. I stared at my phone in disbelief.

By Tuesday afternoon, I still hadn't heard a peep from Jimmy, and it was really starting to freak me out. During English class, I pulled my phone out of my bag and hid it between my copy of *The Scarlet Letter* and the work sheet Mrs. Mason had passed out to us.

I sent Jimmy a message.

Hello, r u mad @ me?

Moments later I got a reply.

No, its fine.
What? Did I say something?
Ten seconds later:
ITS FINE.

ednesday's music rehearsal finished at the same time as Xiang's orchestra one, so she and I ended up sitting on the curb at the edge of the parking lot, waiting for her parents to come pick us up.

I tried to explain my Jimmy problem.

"I've been trying to talk to him, but he keeps insisting he isn't mad. He is, though. I can tell, because within two minutes the conversation grinds to a halt. He pretty much shuts down. How am I supposed to fix a problem that he won't even acknowledge exists?"

"Sorry, I don't get it," she said. "So this all started when he hung up a little suddenly, and now he's less of a Chatty Cathy? Big deal."

"It is a big deal, though!" I insisted. "He's pissed. But can I help it that I don't want to talk about Derek all the time?"

Xiang groaned. "So you *do* know what this is all about, why he's mad."

Yeah. I supposed I did. "Whatever. It's unfair, though," I insisted. "Derek this, Derek that. It's like Jimmy doesn't have anything else in his life to focus on."

Xiang frowned and picked up a pebble from the pavement. "Well, I hardly think we should be throwing stones. We've been *obsessed* with our own boys."

Yeah. I supposed we were.

"And maybe he's mad in part because *you're* not obsessed with Derek," she continued. "Like, he sees you talking to me and Oliver and Kirby and everyone else, and his own personal stuff doesn't take up as much of your attention as it probably would have before you started school here."

"Hmm," I said.

"And, anyway, maybe he really doesn't have anything else to talk about."

"What? Of course he—" I sputtered.

"No, think about it. What did he talk about before he met Derek?"

"He . . . we would talk about *stuff.* Stuff we did, stuff we wanted, people we knew."

"Right. So now he doesn't want to talk about people at his school you don't know, and stuff he's doing without you, and stuff to do with Derek—because you don't like it! Look, sometimes people grow apart."

I physically recoiled from her. "Don't say that! We are not *growing apart.*"

Xiang rolled her eyes. "I'm not saying it's a bad thing! And I'm not saying you're less important to each other. But these things happen, and it's pointless to stress over them. Before, he focused on you. Now it's Derek. And there's only so much you can talk about with this musical. So cut him some slack."

Was it true? Was I Jimmy's Derek, before Derek came along? Maybe my leaving for a different high school had been scarier for him than it had been for me. Is that why he suddenly came out and met a boyfriend? I mean, I'm sure he likes Derek and all, but still . . .

I thought he had joined the musical as a fun, extra way to spend time with me, not as an act of desperation to save our friendship.

"OK, enough about you and your fake problems."

I snapped out of my musing to find Xiang flicking the pebble at me. "Sorry. Yes."

"Let's talk about . . . me!" she said, batting her eyelashes at me.

"OK, gimme the update. How was your rehearsal? Are you finding it easy compared to CYO?"

She thought for a moment. "In some ways yes, in some ways no. It's such a different vibe with a much smaller group. I like that it's more relaxed here, that it's not a lot of stress-y people trying to outdo each other all the time."

"And you sure are getting to see a lot of Parker!" It was true; with CYO on the weekends, she was seeing him almost every other day. "How are things going with that?"

"Well, I was a *bit* nervous about him being here," she said. "I mean, there are only two boys in the orchestra, and you know how boy-crazy everyone is here."

I nodded, remembering the drama-club turnout.

"But it was dumb of me to worry," she said happily. "He's just as oblivious to them as he is to the CYO girls. He's a bit

. . . simple, in that way. And, whatever, I keep him plenty satisfied."

"Eww."

"Oh, lighten up. I'm kidding. But, yeah, you're right, we are seeing way more of each other. It just feels *right*, you know?"

I traced the edge of the curb with my finger, feeling the roughness tickle my skin. "It's not weird with everyone else knowing that you're together? The whole fishbowl effect?"

"Pfffft! Nobody cares!"

Then Xiang became serious, thoughtful. "But I do need to be careful, because one of these days I'm totally gonna forget and say something about him to my parents. It's all become so natural and relaxed, you know?"

No, I wanted to say. Felix made me feel a lot of things, but relaxed was not one of them. But I just sat there, sanding my fingertip on the concrete.

"Dude. Seriously, lighten up." Xiang stood, holding a pack of cigarettes. "And I'm gonna go to that corner over there to do some lighting up of my own. Yell if you see my mom coming. Or a nun."

"You're killing yourself," I sang out to her.

"So be it," she sang back. "But, for reals, you should go easy on Jimmy. After all, he's in looooove!" She grinned and walked away, making kissing sounds.

Rehearsal after school on Thursday was yet another Felix-less one, which was kind of deflating. Opening night was just *eight days* away, and I was spending all my time rehearsing, yet it felt as if he and I had barely spent any time together at all.

I went to get a Twix bar from the snack machine during break. Suddenly a voice behind me said, "Silly Marty. Twix are for kids."

I smiled. "Don't you be judging me, Kaplan," I replied without turning around. But just before I could slide my card into the machine, an unwrapped, solitary Twix bar was dangled in front of me.

"They're perfect for sharing," Oliver said as I accepted his gift. People say that all the time, but let's be honest: who really wants *only one*?

I spun around slowly to see him chomping away at his own bar, his tongue clearly struggling to detach the caramel from his teeth.

"You're doing it all wrong," I said.

"Hmm?"

"Think of it as a sacred procession of flavors."

"Proshession?" he tried to say, smiling through his epic jaw struggle.

"I'm serious," I said. "First, you take a reasonable-size bite. Then you let the chocolate melt. Keep the biscuit and caramel part in the center, between your tongue and the roof of your mouth, so the caramel has nothing to stick to—and that way you don't start thinking about cavities. Feel free to rub the chocolate away from the rest with your tongue. Then the caramel layer will eventually melt, and what you are left with is a biscuit that has reached absolute perfection, a soft, somewhat soggy consistency."

Oliver made an appreciative moan.

"Now, some people don't have the patience to wait for this ideal biscuit to melt, too, which I can understand. But the best things come to those who wait. I happen to know for a fact that it's possible to draw out the biscuit flavor for a solid two minutes."

See? I could do a *great* commercial. Mars, Inc.: Call me!

Oliver managed to swallow enough down to speak properly. "You've clearly given this some thought."

"So all those people who just chomp away at their bars, willy-nilly?" I continued, getting all revved up. "They're crazy. I want to shake them. All that amazing flavor, *totally lost* in giant gulps. And the texture they're experiencing is frankly unpleasant: either sharp, cardboard-y biscuit or unchewable caramel *gum*."

He nodded and tutted in agreement.

"Think about it: There's a reason they don't throw the bars into some blender before packaging them. *A Twix bar is not a salad!*"

"Now, *that* is a T-shirt–worthy slogan if I ever heard one."

"Yes!" I exclaimed. "T-shirts! Billboards! We need to tell the world!"

"Tell the world what?" Jimmy stood in the doorway.

"Hey, my gorgeous garlic clove!" I said, automatically spreading out my arms for a hug.

"Hey," he replied, not returning my smile and, worse, leaving my hug invitation hanging.

Um . . . awkward?

"Jimmy, what is your *deal*?" I asked, exasperated.

Seeing our sudden tension, Oliver jumped in: "Marty has just given me a tutorial on the proper way to eat a Twix bar. Did you know there's a proper technique?"

"Yeah, of *course* I know that," Jimmy said, annoyed. "We developed it together."

Yikes.

"Anyway," he continued, "I just came by to say that Kirby called a few minutes ago, and he can drive us all home later."

"Oh, good, I'll call off my parents," I said, rolling my eyes. "All these silent car rides with them are torture."

"And remember," said Oliver, rubbing his hands together, "I'll be taking my driver's test in just *one week*!"

Jimmy fixed me with a stare. "Since when are you mad at your parents?"

Oh, dear. I had never said anything to Jimmy. "Oh, um, we had a stupid fight a few weeks back. They're giving me a curfew."

"Oh. OK," Jimmy said. Then he turned and walked out.

Oliver looked at me, questioning. "What was that all about?"

"I dunno. He's been weird lately." I chomped on the Twix bar in my hand, which had already started to melt.

It's amazing how time flies, especially when you're doing a show. One minute you're getting your script and working out where to stand, and then all of sudden you look up and you realize that you'll be onstage, performing, in just a few weeks' time. Then you blink, and suddenly it's in a few *days'* time. Don't get me wrong: There's a ton of work in between, but somehow the end of the rehearsal period always comes as a shock.

On the Monday of our opening week, we had one more music-only rehearsal, which Mrs. Murray had organized to keep us focused on getting the notes right. We had been doing the singing in a half-assed way as we worked through the staging and the timing and everything, so we really needed the refresher course.

When she called a short break, the rehearsal room started to empty out. I pulled out my chem homework to see if I could get some of it done, but moments later I realized I wasn't alone. Kate O'Day was sitting in her chair, twirling her pen in one hand and staring at me.

It was very unnerving.

Then she got up and sauntered over. "Do you mind if I give you one tiny piece of unsolicited advice?"

Oh, no. Was she going to criticize my acting or something?

"Make nice with McCafferty. I know she can be a little . . . *much* sometimes, but this play is really important to her."

Wow. Um, not what I was expecting to hear.

"I'm not . . . I mean, I haven't said anything, you know . . . " I stammered, suddenly flushed with shame. Why did she think I was being mean to Jenny? What did I ever do—you know, other than accidently brain her a few weeks ago?

Ah, yes. My Jenny impersonation. Besides nearly killing Chloe on Set Day, it definitely wasn't all that "nice" for Jenny, of course. Oh, man. Now I felt bad. Kate clearly saw me as a Mean Girl.

But, whatever. I was a nobody freshman, while McCafferty was a junior! Why would Jenny even care? And why would popular, senior *Kate* even care? Weren't we all far beneath her notice?

"You haven't said anything directly to her, no," she said, gently grasping my shoulder and letting her eyes crinkle in a show of empathy. "But I think you know what I'm saying. I've seen you roll your eyes at her whenever she talks, imitate her—all that stuff. Jenny—well, she sees it, even if she doesn't let on. You, on the other hand, project your emotions pretty clearly, even if you don't realize it. I think that's part of why you're such a good actor."

OK, now she totally had me stuck. First she accuses me of being mean, and then she wraps the accusation in a compliment, so how am I supposed to defend myself? I just gaped at her, at a loss for words.

Kate gave my arm a little rub and said, "It's just that it can be hard for people who don't fit in so easily. McCafferty only wants good things for us, and I just . . . I don't know. I think that's really cool. We should all embrace her for it."

Some people wandered back into the room, and Kate gave me a quick smile before turning and waltzing back to her seat.

I was totally gobsmacked, so I didn't even notice when, moments later, Felix slid into the chair next to me.

"Sullivan."

"Oh! Peroni."

"Got a question for you." He rubbed his palms together. "What will you be doing tomorrow after school?"

"Tomorrow? Ugh. Going home right after school. Parental lockdown," I said, rolling my eyes, as if otherwise I would be out partying somewhere, like on any other Tuesday in November. (Where? How? With whom?) "How come?"

"Well, I was thinking that you could tell your folks that we're falling behind and that Sister added an extra rehearsal before Wednesday's dress. They wouldn't expect you home for a while, and that would give us some time to, you know, hang out," he said, letting the ambiguity of the phrase pulse between us. Play it cool, Marty.

"I think something like that could be arranged," I said, shifting my weight and folding my arms. It was a pretty good plan, actually; my heinous parents would be none the wiser.

At last, we would be able to spend some actual time together that wasn't just smooching! Not that I'm complaining about the smooching. I'm not.

"Great," he said. "I'll text you the plan later tonight."

That dimple.

hen I got home, I made sure my phone was fully charged. I positioned it in an empty cookie tin (one of many former storage bunkers for Twix bars) so that it would go off like a drum set when Felix's text came. By eleven I was getting drowsy, and at midnight I basically gave in to sleep. It's not like I could text him right back this late; it would be way too obvious that I was waiting for it. I'd have to wait until morning, anyway.

When I woke up, the phone lay in its tray, as silent as ever. No messages.

At breakfast, after explaining to my mother that we had an extra rehearsal that night (and then immediately going back to giving her the silent treatment), I had a total panic attack. OMG, did I leave my phone on some do-not-disturb, non-vibrating, silent mode? After some frantic fumbling in my book bag, I saw that—alas!—all seemed to be in order.

Hmm. Annoying.

Maybe *his* phone had died, and he couldn't find his charger anywhere, and he was going crazy at that exact minute, knowing that I was waiting for his text. Or he mysteriously lost my number?

By second period, I managed to convince myself that he was having trouble making reservations at some special restaurant or something, and he needed to work out a better plan before texting me.

By third period, I started wondering if Felix had changed his mind. I mean, maybe in thinking over on his scenes with Gorgeous O'Day he'd figured he was selling himself short by asking me out?

By fourth period, I was getting worried about Felix. Did he get hit by a tour bus? Abducted by Polynesian terrorists? I mean, if he were found lying in a ditch somewhere, how long would it take before I found out? It's not like anyone would call me. I'd probably only eventually find out in a re-casting announcement from Jenny McCafferty.

By fifth period, I was feeling morose. Who cares about dimples? Boys suck. Maybe I should become a nun, one of those cloistered ones who don't speak and spend all day making Communion bread. I bet they don't shave their legs.

By sixth period, I started wondering if he had promised to text me at all. Had I imagined the entire conversation? Was I losing my grip on reality? I mean, was I totally de-luded, living in a wormhole of my own imagining?

But by the time the last school bell rang, I was livid. Felix could take his phone and shove it up his perfect little butt. I marched up to Xiang and told her I was going to punch Felix's face in the next time I saw him.

"I don't get it. Why don't you just text him?" she asked.

I snorted in response and shook my head. "'Cuz."

"Oh, just do it already."

"Fine." I took my phone out and typed:

???

"That's it? That's all you're going to write?" asked Xiang. "It's all he deserves." Send.

We stared at the phone a moment, riveted, until Xiang broke the spell by snapping her fingers in my face. "Come on, lady. Let's go."

We trudged down the hall, but then my hand honked loudly. Or, at least, the phone in my hand. EEP! It was him! (I had set the phone for the loudest ringtone possible.)

"What'd he say? What'd he say?" asked Xiang, laughing and wrestling for my phone.

"OK, OK, stopstopstopstopstop. You're gonna make me reply by accident—stop it," I said, swatting her away and then holding out the phone for her to read.

SO SRRY CNT DO 2DAY. AFTER REHRSL TMRW? TELL YR PARNTS ITLL BE A L8 1.

"See?" said Xiang. "No big deal."

"But whyyyy?" I whined. "Why is he torturing me like this?"

Xiang put her hands on my shoulders, forcing me to look her in the face. "He's not doing anything," she said, "except spelling terribly. You're the one freaking out. Be cool."

"Oh, I see. Is that how you are with Parker?" I asked accusingly.

Xiang dropped her arms. "Yes. I just snap my fingers, and he comes."

"That's what she said," I blurted out, giggling. Sometimes, yes, I have the maturity level of a ten-year-old.

"Ha-ha."

Just then, my hand/phone started blaring a polka. Ohmigod, was it Felix?

"Hello?"

"Miss Sullivan, I believe you owe me an apology," a male voice said sternly. My heart dropped to the floor. What now?

The voice continued. "I have been waiting for you all day long. It's my birthday, silly! What, don't I get any love?" A huge sigh of relief flooded through me as the voice matched a face in my brain—it was Oliver.

"Oh, my God, Oliver, I didn't recognize your voice! You scared me to death!" I nearly shouted into the phone. Xiang rolled her eyes and wandered away, presumably to smoke.

"Ahem."

"Oh, yes, yes, sorry: Happy birthday! Oh, geez—and you're sixteen! I'm the worst ever. I totally should have called. Happy sixteenth birthday!" OK, now I was yelling. Thank goodness classes were over and the hallway was empty.

"Yep, I'm sixteen all right. And—drumroll, please—a legally licensed driver by the great State of Ohio."

I let out a piercing scream. In most places, that would result in a flood of concerned people rushing out to help someone in need. Not at a girls' school; random screaming is just par for the course. "That's amazing! Totally, totally great. I'm so proud of you! I see that your confidence was well placed."

"Yes, yes, it was. When and where can I pick you up?"

* * * * *

That evening Oliver and I drove around. I mean it: We just *drove*.

"Where should we go?" he asked.

"Dunno. How about ... Lake Erie?"

"Your wish is my command."

And off we went. It's amazing how liberating that is, just picking a random place and going there. No reasons, no schedules, no annoying adults involved. Well, except that we did have to get back by nine, about the time I always got home from rehearsal. And, technically speaking, Oliver had to be back by midnight, since he only had a restricted license until he turned eighteen. Why has no one taken all these restrictions to the Supreme Court? They are so completely unconstitutional. Total age discrimination.

Nevertheless, Oliver was all glow-y. He was so happy, he couldn't stop smiling. I loved that, and his positive energy was totally contagious, completely pushing my Felix melodrama out of mind.

"Come on, come on, let's see it!" I said.

"It's in here," he responded, tossing me his wallet from his door pocket. I pulled out his license. There he was, wide-eyed and grinning like an idiot. But such a cute idiot. His wallet also had a plastic window displaying an old photograph of a youngish woman.

"Your parents must be so proud," I said.

"You have no idea," Oliver said, still shining. "They said I could use this car because they've been planning to get a third one. Getting in and out of our driveway will take some planning, though."

"Is this your mom? She's pretty," I said, indicating the wallet photo. Oliver glanced at it, and his smile wavered slightly.

"Yeah," he said. "But she's . . . gone."

My heart sank in pity. "Oh, Oliver, I'm sorry," I said. "When did she pass away?"

"No, no," he said, laughing. "Gone, like, she left us. I think she's in Utah or somewhere now."

Yikes. Poor Oliver, I thought. I couldn't imagine what that must be like, having your own mom abandon you. I'd be all pissed and, like, burn her picture, not keep it in my wallet.

"Sorry," I said. "I didn't realize."

"Naw, it's all right," he assured me. "I don't really remember her all that much. It was a long time ago. She left me, my little brother, and my dad when I was four."

"Oh, man. Did she . . . like, why did she do it? Did she leave a note or something?"

"She had a lot of problems with drugs and stuff. I don't know all the details; my dad doesn't like talking about it."

"Do you ever miss her?"

"In some strange way, I guess, but I don't really know anything different at this point," he said, keeping his eyes trained on the road. "I mean, I could imagine what it would be like to have her around, and I guess I could miss that, but that's just my fantasy, you know? Maybe we wouldn't have gotten along, or whatever. But the family that I do have is pretty great, and that's enough. I'm really lucky, actually."

I thought about my own parents, about how we definitely didn't have that kind of closeness anymore. I regarded him for a long moment. "You know," I said, "you're a pretty smart guy, knowing what to appreciate. Wiselike."

Oliver flushed crimson, but he flashed me a quick smile. "You're not so dumb yourself," he said.

We drove in contented silence for a while.

"So how's it going with Jenny McCafferty?" I asked.

"Not so bad," he said. "She's intense, but she's actually pretty nice when things settle down."

"Kate said something very similar to that at rehearsal once," I said, regretting not having smoothed things over with Jenny.

"I'm dreading this weekend, though. I can't even imagine how wound up Jenny'll get during final dress rehearsal, let alone opening night."

"It's that soon, isn't it. Just a few days." I shook my head and felt a slight buzz in the pit of my stomach. I would be ready, sure, but *so soon* I would be onstage in front of . . . everyone. Auditions are bad enough, but actual performances really set off my nerves. It's funny how you can both crave and dread something at the same time.

"Derek's really improving," I said. "I was worried about him earlier, but he's becoming a lot more confident."

"Yeah, my boy will be fine," Oliver said. "He never disappoints."

Sunset was approaching, and houses flashed by in quick succession, morphing into different shapes and colors like some kind of suburban flipbook. The houses made me think of HGTV, and that made me think of Jimmy. Jimmy, Jimmy, Jimmy.

"What's your passion, Oliver?" I asked. "I mean, I love that you're doing the play, but it doesn't seem to be the thing that gets you up in the morning."

Oliver gave me a surprised look. "Well, *that's* a pretty hard-core question," he said.

We drove for a minute or so in silence.

"Well, I don't know if you would call it a passion, but I want things to be fair. I guess that's what gets me up in the morning."

It was my turn to be surprised; I figured he would just say Ping-Pong or something.

"Fair?" I asked.

"Yeah, you know? Like justice," he said. "I'll probably end up being a lawyer or an activist. I guess that's partly why I started the GSA at our school. Like, it's crazy that there's no marriage equality in Ohio. It really bugs me when things aren't . . . fair."

"I didn't realize you started that club!" I said, swatting him. "Nobody tells me anything! That's so cool. I'm really proud of you." And I was. I mean, being a gay teenager in suburban Ohio wasn't easy; Jimmy had put up with snide remarks from stupid jerks ever since I'd known him. Oliver probably went through that, too, and then did something about it; he made a space for kids like himself, to make their lives a bit easier.

"I don't know how you have any time for anything," I said, "what with driving lessons, our play, the club, your school newspaper . . ."

"Actually, I quit the *Herald*. I realized I wouldn't be able to do the play at the same time, and, well, it's a lot more fun being around you guys."

"Aww," I said, patting his arm affectionately.

"Oh, I almost forgot!" he said suddenly. "Check out the backseat."

I turned to see that Oliver had drawn one of the seat belts over a small bundle of newspapers. "Go on," he said, "take one."

I managed to pry one loose and smoothed it out on my lap—and drew a sharp breath. It was the *Weeksburg High Herald*, his school newspaper, and plastered all over the front page was Yours Truly. I was laughing, my hair blowing crazily in the breeze, as I completed the word OUT on the cookie tray. The headline screamed, *THE RESULTS ARE IN!* The article was about the school's social-life survey; the caption read, *Making out: 74% of respondents have kissed another student.* Inside were five more of Oliver's pictures from the photo shoot, with similar captions.

"They look really good," I said, smiling.

"Yeah, you make a great cover girl," he said with a wink.

"Oh, stop."

"They kept delaying the article because the administration didn't want to publish the results, but they managed to do it in the end."

"That's awesome," I said. Maybe it was the golden light of dusk, but I felt that the whole world was vibrating with goodness, with promise, somehow.

We soon parked by the bluffs with a view of the lake. The sun was just over the horizon to our left, so I couldn't see his shadowed expression in the glare.

"So. Lake Erie," he said.

"Yup." I nodded. "Lake Erie." The moment hung there to be savored.

"Come on, let's feel it," I said, breaking the spell and launching us out of the car.

We stood in the bracing autumn wind and looked out over the dark expanse of water before us. It seemed as if the whole lake was slowly rocking back and forth with every wave.

Oliver placed his hand over mine, and I leaned against his shoulder. "I'm glad you're here," he said. Our fingers intertwined.

"Me, too," I said. "Me, too."

A t home, I had an e-mail from Jimmy waiting for me in my inbox: *Call me!!*

Dutiful as always, I dialed his number. It rang four or five times before a girl's voice answered, *"Klausau!"*

I was flabbergasted. "Uh, is this—did I dial—uh, Jimmy?"

"Aišku, aš nesu Jimmy."

Wait a minute. I knew that voice. "Jeanie? Is that you?"

Silence.

"Jeanie, please give Jimmy back his phone."

I heard fumbling, then Jimmy's voice in the background. "Give it! Now get out!"

"Sorry," he said, breathing heavily. "Jeanie got to my phone before I did."

"Was she speaking some kind of . . . ?"

"Yeah, she's teaching herself Lithuanian. Don't ask," he said irritably. "So what's up?"

"I don't know. You're the one who summoned me," I reminded him.

"Oh! Right!" he said, surprisingly chipper. "We need to talk. I was talking to Derek earlier, and he told me the most *interesting* thing."

Oh, Lord. More about Derek? Really? Was he just going to act like things hadn't been weird between us?

"And where were you, by the way?" he continued. "I called before, and your parents said you were at rehearsal. But you and I both know *that's* not true."

"Oliver got his license today, and we went for an inaugural drive to Lake Erie."

There was a long pause. "Lake Erie?"

"Yeah. Lake Erie," I said, smiling at the memory. "Oliver is a really interesting guy. Did you know that his mom ran out on his family when he was little? And that he actually started the gay club they're in at Weeksburg High?"

There was another long pause.

"What? Jimmy, are you still there?"

"Look, I'm just gonna say it. Why didn't you tell me you were going?"

Oh, man. *Was Jimmy jealous of Oliver?*

Ugh, it all made sense: Jimmy thought Oliver was becoming my new GBF! That explained Jimmy's extra-frostiness when he'd walked in on me and Oliver at the snack machine. He thought I was replacing him with a cuter model. One with a driver's license, no less.

"The drive was just a spur-of-the-moment thing. It wasn't, like, planned."

"Right. But planned enough to lie to your parents about it."

"That was because I was *supposed* to go out with Felix."

"Oh, really! Well! That's news. And then you decided to go out with Oliver instead. And telling me about any of these things didn't even cross your mind."

"It wasn't like that. Felix—"

"Look," he said. "If this is how you want things to be, fine. I just thought we were better friends than that. Stupid me."

I sighed, and thought, OH, MY GOD, HE IS SUCH A DRAMA QUEEN.

"You're blowing things way out of proportion," I said, annoyed that I had to humor his need for affirmation. "We *are* good friends. We're *best* friends."

"It's not feeling like it."

Oh, Lord. "Well, it should. Now. Tell me what interesting thing Derek told you earlier."

Jimmy snorted. "Never mind. It doesn't matter. It's fine."

Click.

There was that word again—*fine*. Clearly, it was anything but.

Something strange had happened tonight: I wasn't sure where my loyalties were anymore. I mean, despite this stupid fight, Jimmy would always be my oldest friend. But already I felt that Oliver was perhaps becoming . . . a closer friend? Somehow I acted different when I was alone with Oliver, in a way that felt deeper, more genuine. Maybe I was growing up, and my relationship with Jimmy remained stuck in who we both used to be.

Well, whatever. I sighed heavily and flopped onto my bed.

Enough of the gay-boy dramas. I had my first real date tomorrow! Felix and I were grabbing dinner after rehearsal.

Finally.

*Y*owza! My first date ever!

Here's how it went down.

Well, first of all, the dress rehearsal went on and on. Everyone (including me) was getting nervous about the upcoming opening, so we were all hyper and distracted. That, of course, meant that we kept wasting time, missing cues, and screwing up lines.

But the biggest distraction was the costumes. Calliope had done an amazing job, not surprisingly—we all looked phenomenal. I realized she had been asking about my head movement because she had added a wire armature inside the hood to lift it above my hair, like some kind of astronaut's helmet. It looked cool, but it totally restricted my peripheral view, leaving me like a horse with blinders, so I managed to convince her to take the wire out and leave it as a normal hood. I mean, this play was going to be complicated enough without my being visually impaired.

Felix's Wolf outfit was the most impressive. Just like in the Broadway show, he had a fake muscle-y chest—not that Felix needed that kind of enhancement, in my opinion. But he did look a lot older and hairier, with Wolverine-like claws, so it was a bit unnerving to have him advance toward me, snarling, in our big number together.

Look at that flesh,
Pink and plump.
Hello, little girl . . .

His Cinderella's Prince costume, on the other hand, made him look like something out of a Disney cartoon. Swoon!

But as I said, the performance was a mess. Even reliably sunny Sister Mary Alice was reaching her limits, which in her case meant stony silences and long looks that only made you wish she would scream at you or throw things instead.

"I'm not going to raise my voice," she'd say, all low and warbly, "but you should remember that at seven thirty on Friday evening there will be a reckoning. Will it be a triumph? Or a painful, regrettable disaster? It's up to you."

Her surgically precise guilt trips were in sharp contrast to Jenny's broad reign of bossiness backstage. Poor Oliver and Jimmy bore the heaviest onslaught of commands as they scurried back and forth, putting out fires—ripped costumes here, off-kilter spotlights there, dead microphones everywhere. Jenny was running around, too, issuing endless reprimands to the cast, which inspired a staggering range of curses in response. Everyone was on edge.

Except for Kate O'Day, that is, who was an island of tranquil professionalism. She paid attention and never missed her cues, and she blatantly ignored anyone who tried whispering when we were supposed to be silent. It seemed a bit stuck-up at first, but by the end of the rehearsal she had pretty much shamed us all into some semblance of sober focus.

After sitting through Sister Mary Alice's and Mrs. Murray's scathing notes, we were finally released. It was late, about ten o'clock, so everyone left right away. Luckily, my parents understood that the rehearsal was bound to run really late, so I didn't have to worry about curfew. Oliver had offered me a ride with him and Derek earlier, but, without thinking, I'd told him I was going to grab a late dinner with Felix.

"Oh?" he replied, clearly taken aback.

"It's not . . . like . . . ," I said, flailing for words. I should have told him about Felix by now, I realized.

"It's OK. You don't have to—I mean, it's fine," he said, giving me a quick smile before walking off to meet Derek.

Felix had texted Matt (remember him? The spiky-blond jock from the audition?) to pick us up, so we ended up standing in the parking lot to wait. It was getting cold already, so there were no fireflies or droning crickets to give any indications of life in the landscape. Only one fluorescent lamp fixture unsteadily pooled light on the asphalt around us, with just the inky void beyond. Watching the tiny red dots of car taillights recede into the darkness, I momentarily regretted having not taken Oliver up on the offer of a ride. I was tired, and it would have been nice just to get into his cozy car with him, like yesterday. With him and Derek, I mean.

Felix sat down on the ground and patted the curb.

OK, this was a pretty attractive option, too.

I plopped down. His arm snaked over my shoulders, and I worried that he could feel my heart banging against my rib cage. I took a deep breath and slowly exhaled, opening my eyes to gaze at the starlit sky above.

"Pretty intense day, huh?" he asked.

"Yeah," I answered, searching for something more to say but coming up short.

"Sorry about last night. My grandmother wasn't doing so great, so I couldn't really get away."

I thought about the old woman at the mall and how she clearly had health issues. And to think I was being such a jerk about not hearing from him all day yesterday, while he had something way more important to focus on.

"No need to explain," I said, chastened. "It's OK."

So, instead, we kissed. And kissed. Eventually a black Camaro roared into the parking lot and swerved to a screeching halt, its tires drawing parentheses on the asphalt.

Felix whooped and sprang up. The doors on either side of the car opened, and Matt and a girl with frizzy black hair and a glitzy miniskirt stepped out.

"Hi, I'm Brianna," she said, giving me a once-over. "You must be Mary."

"Martha," I corrected her.

"Oh, right, sorry," she said, in no way apologetically.

"Dude, let's roll. I'm starvin'," Matt said. I climbed into the back with Felix, where the seats were apparently designed for small monkeys, not humans. An empty soda cup crushed against my foot as Brianna ratcheted her seat into me.

"You got enough room back there?" she asked.

"Yep, all set," I said, wondering whether the fact that I couldn't move an inch in any direction would actually help me in an accident or mean certain death.

Felix didn't have it any better, but it was nice to be able to just *hold hands* for once—a welcome distraction from Matt's NASCAR-inspired driving style. Eventually he pulled into the Friendly's off I-71, just north of Weeksburg. We went inside, grabbed a booth, and ordered some properly greasy food. Actually, I ordered greasy food first, and Matt joined me, and then Felix and Brianna ordered sensible salads. (Dating lesson learned.)

So it turned out that Brianna didn't really know the guys that well; she was going out with Matt for the first time.

"So what school do you go to?" I asked.

"Holy Name," she replied, delicately spearing a cucumber slice with her fork.

"Oh, so do you know Felix's sister? What's her name again?" I asked, turning to Felix.

"Jill. Jill Peroni," he said. "She's a senior. Do you know her?"

Brianna thought for a moment but then shook her head and shrugged. "Peroni? I know some Jills but no Peronis. I don't know that many seniors, really, but I've probably met her at some point."

"So how did you meet Matt?" Felix asked her.

Brianna went into this long, complicated story involving mixed-up movie tickets at the mall, with Matt grunting his agreement occasionally as he ate. Felix's eyelids fluttered and started to droop, and he yawned widely, arching his back and stretching his elbows up in the air. His shirt lifted, and I caught a glimpse of his stomach, lean and toned. Damn, he was good-looking.

Brianna had moved on to another story, this time involving something that had happened to her friend Shawna's brother. I was trying to focus, but Felix's sleepiness proved totally contagious. It didn't help that the restaurant was about a billion degrees hot. Felix caught my eye and winked in sympathy, then patted my knee under the table. I drained the last of my Coke, hoping the caffeine and sugar would get me through Brianna's next topic: how her neighbor's dog farted all the time.

Felix's hand remained on my leg.

"... and then I said to her, 'Who the hell do you think you are, bumping me with your baby carriage?'" Brianna droned on, and Felix shifted in his seat. As he did so, his hand slid farther up my thigh.

His hand suddenly seemed a lot less charming. I felt the room wobble oppressively.

"... the whole thing was totally ridiculous. I mean, what the hell makes her so special? I was, like, this close to ..."

I was frozen in place. I mean, what was I supposed to do? What, exactly, was Felix up to—I mean, we were in the middle of freakin' Friendly's, for God's sake!

His hand crept farther, almost to my crotch, and a wave of nausea washed over me.

The waitress walked by, and I shot out of the booth, following her.

"Where are the restrooms?"

I pushed open the door and practically collapsed, grabbing onto the sink for support. I splashed my face with cold water, then stared hard at my unsteady reflection, trying to get control of myself. I was breathing really hard, but somehow I couldn't get enough air. What had just happened? Why was I reacting this way? How had I gone from making out with Felix and being, like, "look at his abs" to suddenly feeling so . . . violated?

All I wanted to do now was go home. Just go home and curl up in bed. Be anywhere but here.

I cradled my cell phone, considering my options.

There is one very big drawback to being a really good, upstanding person: No one ever wants to disappoint you. I
know that sounds like a good thing at first—I mean, Sister
Mary Alice used that impulse to great effect in the musical,
getting us all to work hard and do our best. But sometimes
you need people who understand you. Obviously not my
parents, who thought I was at rehearsal, anyway. I didn't
call Jimmy—I didn't even know where we stood anymore.
And I didn't call Xiang. (Of course, what could Jimmy or
Xiang have even done—asked their parents to come pick
me up from Friendly's? But, whatever, I'm trying to make
a point here.)

And I didn't call Oliver, either. Now, don't get me wrong:
It's not that I thought he would have been all judgmental.
And in my head, I knew that there wasn't anything to be
ashamed about. But I still *felt* that way, like somehow I had
totally gotten myself into this situation with Felix, and that
I'm such an immature weirdo for not knowing how to deal
with it gracefully. I mean, I was sure that someone else—
anyone else—would have known what to do. Hell, probably
anybody else would have welcomed Felix's advances and
matched them. What was wrong with me, that I was having such a strong, basically physical reaction to something

that, really, was no big deal? Why couldn't my brain stop my heart from racing or my palms from sweating?

I called Kirby. Somehow I just knew that he would understand. That he wouldn't ask questions. That when I asked him to pick me up, he'd hear what I was really saying. That he'd come, and he'd find a way to get me the hell out of there.

And that's exactly what he did.

I went back to the booth, where Matt and Brianna were flicking fries at each other and snorting with laughter.

Felix fixed me with a questioning stare. "So, are you feeling OK?" he asked.

"Oh, yeah, I guess," I said, fumbling for a convincing explanation for my long absence and coming up short. "I kind of have a headache. It's been such a long day." (When in doubt, try a cliché!)

He patted the booth next to him, and I slunk into a seated position. He put his arm around me, and I'm sure he meant it to be sympathetic and protective, but it only made me feel trapped.

What was wrong with me? How had my feelings for this guy turned so quickly? And how long would it take for Kirby to get here?

Thankfully, not too long—the Friendly's wasn't too far from Weeksburg High, where Kirby, Oliver, and Derek all went to school. I saw Kirby enter, and relief flooded through me. He first walked toward the bathroom but then backtracked when he spotted our booth.

I suddenly had the horrifying realization that I hadn't thought to discuss a cover story with him. I mean, it would be totally obvious to my dinner companions that I'd called him from the bathroom, and that would be super-bizarre, right?

But Kirby is a pro. When he got within a few feet of me he feigned surprise—really convincingly; he totally should have auditioned!—and busted out with, "Holy shit, Marty? What the hell are you doin' out here?"

I reddened, paralyzed.

But he didn't wait for an answer. He came over and introduced himself to the others. "Hey, I'm Kirby. I live down the street from Marty here." He turned to me. "Hey, yo, how are you gettin' home? I'm just leaving. You need a ride?"

Oh, hallelujah. "Actually, that's a great idea!" I said brightly. I sprang out of the booth, turning to the others and saying, "Sorry, guys. This has been great, but I'm totally bushed. Here's a twenty—that should cover me."

And—boom—we were out of there.

Kirby and I didn't speak the whole way home. Once I tried, saying, "Kirby, look—" but he cut me off.

"Stop. It's OK."

So I settled back in my seat and exhaled.

When he pulled up to my house, it was getting close to midnight, which was stretching what my parents would find believable for a very late rehearsal. One more reason I was glad I'd left Friendly's when I did.

Kirby turned off the engine.

"Look, I'm the last person in the world who should be giving advice about anything," he said, all quiet and subdued, staring at the steering wheel. "It's a lot easier to log on to a Web site and send some chat messages than it is to deal with real people in real life. I know that."

Then he turned to look directly at me and held my gaze. "But it doesn't have to be hard, either. If things don't feel right to you, they probably aren't."

I smiled weakly in response.

"Thanks for—you know," I said, and I got out.

There was one good thing about the humongous-disaster-that-was-my-first-date: It took my mind off the musical . . . a bit.

Actually, that's a lie. It didn't take my mind off the musical at all.

How was it that I could stress and obsess with my whole body and soul about what I could possibly say to Felix the next day that in any way made sense, yet *also* stress and obsess with my whole body and soul about the performance on Friday? It was as if my capacity for nervousness had doubled all of a sudden. Not good.

The next day was our final dress rehearsal, the last chance to screw up our lines, our blocking, or our cues without ruining our lives forever. It's bad enough looking like a jackass in front of thirty people you've been working with for months—and screwing up the thing they've been working just as hard on. But it's so much worse when the entire school, basically, and all your family and friends—and enemies—are there watching. Oh, and recording it all, to make sure your grandchildren will also be able to ridicule you until the day you die.

I got a text from Felix during Mr. Dartagnan's class.

U SEEMED A LTTL OUT OF IT LAST NITE. R WE OK?

Almost out of habit, I passed my phone to Xiang. She passed it back and didn't say anything; she just gave me a concerned look.

I suddenly regretted showing her the message. I like melodrama, not pity; there's a difference.

At lunch, she cut right to the chase. "So spill. What happened 'last night'?" She literally did air quotes with her fingers.

"Oh, nothing. I don't even know why I showed you that. I was just tired last night." I took a big gulp of soy milk.

"Tired," she said. "On your first real, *public* date with Felix Peroni, a boy you've been obsessing over for weeks."

"I just . . . I dunno. I just—" And suddenly tears were streaming down my face.

Xiang sprang into action, grabbing my arm and dragging me away from my lunch, out of the cafeteria, and into the nearest restroom.

She checked to make sure all the stalls were empty, then sat me down on the radiator.

I was a full-blown mess by this point, all red-faced and shuddering.

"What. Happened."

"We went to Friendly's, that's all," I choked out. "With his friend Matt and some girl from Holy Name. At some point Felix just . . . got . . . you know, affectionate. Frisky."

"Be specific." Xiang was stone serious.

"He put his hand on my leg. And moved it up a little. No big deal."

"Well, it's a big deal if it makes you cry at lunch, Marty," she pressed. I had never seen Xiang like this—no zingers, no sarcasm.

"I'm just tired. And stressed about the musical. It's nothing."

"It's not *nothing*, Marty," she shot back. "You obviously didn't want him to do that. You weren't ready."

In retrospect, I'm sure Xiang meant that in a supportive way, but something about the way she said *ready* rubbed me the wrong way. Like because she smokes cigarettes or is someone who does more than just kiss, that means she's way more sophisticated than me? When I thought about it, she was always full of advice, lecturing me, telling me why people are the way they are and how I should act.

I flailed my arms. "What the hell does that mean? *You're* almost having sex. Why wouldn't *I* be 'ready'?"

Xiang reared back. "Whoa. This isn't about me, Marty. This is about you. Actually, it's about Felix." She did an eye-roll maneuver. "It's not some *competition*."

My tears were still flowing, and somehow all my swirling emotions had channeled themselves into anger. Embarrassed, frustrated, confused rage.

"You know what? Fuck you," I said, pushing past her and back into the cafeteria. I grabbed my abandoned lunch as I passed our table, dropping it into the garbage on my way out. In the parking lot, I pulled out my phone.

Sorry about last nite, just a weird combo of exhaustion and nerves. We're gr8. CU soon. xoxo.

Send.

When I walked into Jerry Hall for rehearsal a few classes later, Xiang was already in the orchestra pit, giggling over something with Parker. Her eyes met mine, and she froze. I could feel her gaze follow me as I walked up to Felix and wrapped my arms around him, drawing him into a big ol' French kiss.

As we broke away from each other, Felix was left with a wolfish grin, and his hand lingered on my hip.

Not ready, my ass, I thought to myself.

As I looked around, it became clear that our PDA had surprised everyone. Not just Xiang and Jimmy, who knew our secret, but Oliver and Kate and Jenny McCafferty—and Sister Mary Alice, who for once looked truly at a loss for words. Was it really such a shock, Felix and me together?

Jenny ended the awkward moment, clearing her throat loudly. "All right, people—places. This is the final run-through, so it has to be flawless. Flaw. Less."

We shuffled off backstage, and Felix kept his hand on my waist. He pulled me into a corner behind the curtain and pressed himself against me, kissing me deeply.

"Well, I guess we're out now," he breathed. "You are so hot today."

"Oh," I said, "about last night—"

"No worries," he said. "Let's just enjoy the time we've got left."

My miscomprehension must have shown, because he smiled broadly. "In the musical. The time left together here in the show." With a quick nibble on my ear, he bounded out of our corner toward the stairs to the dressing rooms.

Suddenly Jimmy was at my side, pulling on my elbow.

"What was *that*?" he hissed.

"Excuse me?"

"It's like I don't even know you. Why would you go and do *that*?"

"I can hear the words leaving your mouth, but I have no idea what you are saying."

The overhead lights flashed twice, Jenny's signal for the show start.

Jimmy held both his palms up in front of my face. "Whatever. I can't deal with this—with you—right now," he said and then sprinted off to the sound booth.

I stood there, stunned. I didn't know what to think. Yes, I'd made out with Felix. Big deal! He makes out with Derek all the time! And he knew I'd hooked up with Felix before, so was this just because it was in front of other people?

AARGH. Like I don't have enough drama right now

with the show and Xiang probably never speaking to me again. Shake it off, Marty, I told myself as I headed to wardrobe.

But just before I got to the bottom of the stairs, Oliver appeared, blocking my path.

"Hey," he said. He didn't look too happy, but I couldn't really be sure, since his face was deeply shadowed by the light pouring out from behind him.

"Hi. What's up? Shouldn't you be at the curtain controls? Jenny will totally—"

"Yeah, I know. But this'll be quick. I saw you . . ." He flailed his arms. "You know, with Felix. And I don't want to tell you what to do, but I just . . . I don't think you've really thought this through."

Oh, Lordy.

"You, too?" I asked, hand on hip. "First Xiang is all patronizing; then Jimmy gets all pissy. Jesus Christ, what is going on here? I can't win! I'm so sick of this shit," I said, trying to move past him. But Oliver held out an arm, blocking me.

"You deserve better, Marty. He's an asshole." I had never heard Oliver swear before, and it seemed really unfair that he would be criticizing Felix without really knowing him—and criticizing me, too, basically, for hooking up with him.

"Excuse me, but where do you get off telling me what the hell I should do?"

He flinched and stepped back as if I'd slapped him.

Whatever. "I'm late," I huffed, moving past him before angry tears formed.

In the dressing room, I managed to calm down and text my mom.

All my rides fell through 2nite. You have 2 pick me up at 11.

An unexpected benefit to having weird drama in your life? You get better at drama (like, theater drama), because it's sooo nice to leave yourself for a while. When I was onstage that night, with all the costumes and the lighting and the scenery, I *was* Little Red Riding Hood. All the rehearsals finally clicked into place, and I easily made all my cues. Even in my one scene with Felix, I wasn't thinking about Felix—it was just the lurid Wolf following me through the woods. And when I sang my big solo about, well, life, I was still Red. I was someone who had never heard the name Martha Sullivan—or met her totally critical, judgmental, unsupportive, so-called friends—in an enchanted forest no-where near Nowhere, Ohio.

That night I lay in bed for hours just staring at the ceiling. (If you're wondering about the wisdom in that, you're right: If you have a super-important event the next day—say, the opening night of a musical in which you will sing in front of hundreds of people—it's not a good idea to add sleep deprivation to your list of concerns.)

My mom had seen the Hsus' car in the parking lot when she had come to pick me up. On the drive back she had asked, "Are you and Xiang not getting along?"

All she got in response was "None of your business."

And I don't know what this says about me, but I wasn't all torn up over my fight with Xiang, my only true friend at school. And I wasn't even bothered about Jimmy, my onetime BFF, being all mad at me. I had a grinding, scissors-y feeling in my chest, and I just couldn't stop picturing Oliver's big brown eyes as I pushed past him. They were so sad. No, not sad. Disappointed. Hurt.

Jimmy and Xiang were probably jealous of me and Felix, since both of their boyfriends have the personality of a cardboard box. But what made Oliver think Felix was an asshole? Felix was vain, yes, and certainly not subtle when he wanted something. He was loud and confident and ridiculously hunky—everyone thought so.

Even if I could justify everything in my head, the churning didn't stop in my chest. I lay awake—wide awake—rubbing a river pebble as if it were a rosary bead.

So the next day at school was exactly the nightmare you would it expect it to be. I was groggy from the lack of sleep, physically numb from nerves over the show—literally, my hands were cold and tingly—and in the pissiest mood ever because of my ex-friends. I studiously avoided speaking to or making eye contact with Xiang during math, and I ate my lunch in the parking lot. (Actually, I ate a third of my lunch. I had approximately zero appetite.) I totally failed a pop quiz during chemistry because I couldn't think straight, and then I forgot my copy of *The Scarlet Letter* in my locker, which meant that in English I had to look on with this girl who—I'm not going to say her name, so I don't get sued or something—totally does not understand personal hygiene. Even after class ended, I kept sniffing myself, wondering whether it was possible for BO to be transmitted to others by air currents or something. Not cool.

After classes, we still had a few hours before curtain, so Sister Mary Alice and Mrs. Murray summoned the whole cast and crew to Jerry Hall in order to address last-minute "weaknesses" in the show. They had ordered a bunch of pizzas and left them for us to graze on in the lobby, and it quickly became clear that nervous girls don't eat, while nervous boys eat like there's no tomorrow. Jimmy, Oliver, and Derek lingered near the food in a tight huddle, glancing over at me every now and then. I couldn't tell if they were pissed at me or scared of me. Anyway, I was sitting with Felix on a radiator; he was scarfing a slice with one hand, his other arm draped over my shoulders.

How did this even happen, that I went from having all these friends to . . . this? Well, at least Felix was here with me, and I tried to take comfort from his protective arm weighing down on me. It was a pretty heavy arm.

I sipped a Coke absentmindedly, but then the sugar rush made me feel nauseous, so I stopped. I had to pee, and my butt was getting hot, but I figured I'd try to hold it as long as possible so I wouldn't have to go, like, a dozen times before the show started. (Let's not deconstruct that logic, OK?)

During notes, Sister Mary Alice and Mrs. Murray didn't have too much to say about me, so I sat in a middle row by myself while Foster, who played the role of Jack, redid his solo about a billion times. He kept screwing up the pacing. I looked over and saw Derek stooped over, with his head clasped in white-knuckled hands.

Even in the midst of my own turbulent hell, I could see that Derek's was worse. Poor guy.

Felix, on the other hand, seemed totally *not* nervous. He was already wearing his shaggy gray Wolf suit, without the mask, so he looked like a hot half-Muppet. Even after my weird reaction on Wednesday, I still thought he was the most attractive person I'd ever seen.

I glanced over at Oliver farther down my row, but he just

looked straight ahead at Foster, uncharacteristically serious. Cold as ice.

Whatever. There were only forty minutes left before the
show, and I had other things to focus on. Mainly, not throwing up.

In the girls' dressing room, I found something poking out
of my duffel bag. It was a folded invitation from Maria Kilkenny for the cast party at her house on Saturday night. On
it she had scribbled, *And be ready for our drunken "Memory"
duet!!!* Next to the invitation was a handmade card. Earlier,
during the pizzas, I had seen Maria working in a back corner of the auditorium by herself, and I realized she must
have made individual cards for everyone in the cast. Why
didn't I think to do something like that?

Mine featured a pressed, dried flower glued to the cover.
Inside was written in silver marker:

> *Take extra care with strangers,*
> *Even flowers have their dangers,*
> *And though scary is exciting,*
> *Nice is different than good.*

Aww, so cute! The lyric was from my big song in the first
act. This was such a thoughtful gesture, and it made me
wonder why I hadn't gotten to know Maria better during
these past couple of months. She was funny! And theater-y!
Maybe this blowup with Xiang and the guys was the best

thing that could have happened to me, you know? Opened up my eyes to the people around me.

I walked over to Maria and enveloped her in a proper hug, to the point where she seemed a bit taken aback. (People should hug more often and with gusto, so it doesn't come as a shock.)

"The party tomorrow will be amazing," I said. "I'm so excited."

"Um, great! See you there," she replied, recovering from my sudden outpouring of love.

I double-checked my makeup in the mirror, carefully laced up my red cape, and headed out to my position in the wings. Oh, wait—was there enough time for a final bathroom visit? Yeah, I could make it.

You know the sound of an audience quieting down, just before a show is supposed to start? First it's the happy clatter of hundreds of people talking, then a slow ebb as people see the lights go down, and then just the last holdouts finishing their frantic, whispered conversations. As the ambient volume faded, I felt the pit of my stomach lift, as if I was suddenly released into free fall. And for the next two and a half hours, I would be at terminal velocity.

Curtain up.

Performances, especially opening-night performances, are totally different from even the most polished of final run-through dress rehearsals. Sister Mary Alice had recruited a bunch of seniors to sit and watch our last rehearsal, just so we would feel the pressure of an audience and start adjusting to their laughs and applause (and hopefully not their boos and rotten tomatoes). Even so, it wasn't quite the same thing as a *performance*. From the first words spoken, something magical happens. It's incredible how a bit of lighting, a few costumes, and some music can really take you somewhere else—in this case, the fantasy world of fairy tales. But, really, I think it's the audience that does it. They expect to be somewhere else, and, well, that seems to be enough. Together, we all go there.

During the first number, after I'd ordered the cakes and bread for Granny at the Baker's and while Cinderella cast her spell on the birds, I had a few moments onstage in the dark. I looked out at the crowd, no longer blinded by the lights, and saw Jimmy's family first. Actually, I saw Jeanie first, since she was wearing a huge, sparkly turban. And was that a *toga* she was wearing? Um, yeah, looked like it. Jimmy's parents were seated on either side of her, and farther down the row I saw my own parents, my father's round glasses reflecting the lit stage like headlights on a vintage car. A few rows back were Xiang's mom and dad, and just behind them was Matt, Felix's friend. I didn't see Brianna with him; instead, he was sitting with a brunette. It took me a second to recognize her as Jill, Felix's sister. She looked a lot older without her Holy Name uniform.

I caught sight of Kirby in the mass of people, and next to him was a redheaded man who must have been his dad. Next to *him* was Oliver's dad—I could just make out his cropped gray hair and goatee—and my smile dimmed. I had just been getting to know Oliver before all this crap blew up. He had said that he didn't miss having his mom around, but . . . still. I wondered whether he missed her at events like these.

Would we ever be friends again?

Oops—Jack was finishing up his scene with the cow, and I was up next.

During Act Two, Felix slid up next to me backstage and gave me a quick peck on the cheek. "Lookin' good out there," he whispered, with a wink. That dimple would be the death of me.

"You, too," I responded, tracing his jawline with my index finger. He must not have been expecting it, because he winced a bit. We were in a corner, blocked off by fake trees nailed onto rolling platforms, so we were covered in dappled shadows, like camouflage. He was wearing his Prince outfit, and he could have just walked out of a romance novel. My hand searched out his in the darkness and gave it an affectionate squeeze.

He pulled me close with one arm, and he turned and pressed against me, his other hand resting on my hip. He drew me into a kiss, his soft lips smothering the maelstrom of thoughts swirling in my head. Ohhhh, hello . . .

Then his tongue started pushing into my mouth, and I realized his left hand had migrated up from my hip to my right breast.

The room started pulsing, and the blizzard of thoughts

returned. Eesh—what was he doing? His fat tongue filled my mouth, and I could feel my throat constricting. When was my next cue onstage? His hand was mashing my boob, clenching and unclenching, and I could feel the lacing of my cape strain against my neck. This should be pleasant, right? Where was everyone else? I leaned back, but he leaned farther forward and pulled his hand harder against the small of my back. What was wrong with me? Did I smell fries?

A wave of nausea slammed into me, and I instinctively pushed Felix away. He staggered back into the branches of a fake tree.

"What the *fuck*?" he spat at me.

"I . . . just . . . bathroom . . ." I pushed past him and, clawing in the darkness, stumbled toward the dressing rooms.

I tripped, and as I pitched forward I thought I heard Felix hiss, *"Bitch."*

But just as I was about to hit the ground, I felt someone grab my arm to support me. I sank to my knees and looked up to see Jenny McCafferty standing over me. The room swayed.

"One sec," Jenny said. Moments later a bucket materialized in front of me. My body convulsed, and I vomited.

"It's OK. Just breathe," Jenny whispered, rubbing my back. "It's gonna be fine."

J enny managed to steer me into the girls' bathroom, where I was able to clean up.

"It must be nerves," I gasped, and she just nodded. I splashed my face with cold water.

She glanced down at her watch.

"Oh!" I cried. "You've got to—"

"It's OK," she repeated. "My two assistants are handling things. I just want to be sure you're all set."

"Yeah, I'm OK, really. I can go back. Like I said, it was just—"

"Nerves. Right," Jenny said.

"I'm fine. Really. Thanks for . . ." I waved my arm, indicating, well, everything.

We stood there for a moment in silence, and eventually she took a step back toward the door.

"OK, then," she said. "I think you've got about one minute left before you need to be stage right." She gave me one more concerned look before slipping out the door.

Then the door opened a second later, and she walked back in. She pulled a Twix bar from her pocket and laid it on the counter. "Not for right now, obviously, but for later. When you feel up to it."

Then she was gone again.

I realized, too late, that I hadn't made things right with Jenny. I really should have, after Kate's little talk. On the other hand, it seemed kind of cruel to try to apologize for my impersonations; I mean, would it embarrass Jenny to have to acknowledge the fact that people make fun of her?

Well, it seemed Jenny had forgiven me anyway, but that only increased my guilt. I grabbed the Twix bar and twisted halfheartedly at its packaging, but then decided against opening it; I was definitely still in the nausea danger zone. I put it down on the counter and stared hard at myself in the mirror.

Marty, pull it together.

Thankfully, Little Red Riding Hood's biggest singing moments in the show were already done, and the rest of the act passed uneventfully. I basically just had to stay onstage and listen to other people sing around me. But when the curtain went down, the whistling from the audience still buzzing in my head, I knew I had to talk to Felix. Was he pissed at me? He must have been really confused, just as I was, about how I'd reacted. Should I just make something up, tell him I had food poisoning or something?

And did he *really* call me a bitch, or did I mishear him? Maybe we both had some explaining to do.

Behind the curtain, Sister Mary Alice, weighed down by the massive bouquet the cast and crew had presented to her at curtain call, delivered a totally heart-melting speech ("triumphant success," "proved to the board that you can do pretty much anything," "a pleasure and, more important, an honor, to work with you"). Soon everyone was going around giving one another celebratory hugs, and after extracting myself from Kate O'Day's narrow arms and teary smile, I saw Felix, still dressed as a prince, ducking out of the backstage area and into the lobby. I followed, hurrying to catch up, but the audience had already started pouring in from the auditorium.

I called out his name, but he didn't hear, and soon we were both swallowed by the crowd. A man wearing black jeans and a dark V-neck tee stopped in front of me, blocking my progress.

"Miss Sullivan," he said. "Magnificent work. What a pleasant surprise."

It took me a second to recognize Mr. Dartagnan, my math teacher. Without his baggy khaki pants and loud ties, he was like Dr. Jekyll to his Mr. Hyde.

"Thanks, Mr. Dartagnan," I replied, nodding and smiling and edging past him. Then I heard someone calling my name to my left, and I turned to see my parents pushing their way toward me. My mom thrust a bunch of pink roses at me, and they both beamed.

"What a great show. You were marvelous!" she cried.

"Thanks," I replied, gamely accepting the flowers. It was hard to be mad at them while they were so clearly delighted with me.

"Great job, kiddo," said my dad as he squeezed my shoulder.

I went up on tiptoe, trying to spot Felix over people's heads.

"I'll be right back," I said, and I dove into the stream of people making its way out the doors. I caught a brief glimpse of Felix's royal-blue jacket just before he turned down the hallway leading to the back entrance. But just before I reached the hallway, I heard someone bellow,

"YOU!"

I turned to see Jeanie, fully decked out in her turban-and-toga garb. Both her arms were raised toward me, and she had a crazed, wide-eyed expression. I saw now that this look was exaggerated by white pancake makeup on her face and heavy black kohl applied around her eyes; she looked more stage-ready than I did.

"Jeanie, hey. Good to see you," I mumbled uncertainly. She took an exaggerated step toward me.

"You!" she repeated, starting to wave her arms wildly. "The spirit of Ahm-al-Aknour, Vice-Sultan of Upper Phoenicia, has a message for you."

"Jeanie, I don't have time right—"

"*Regret!* You shall soon be plagued with great regret!" she hissed.

"Um, OK, thanks for the message. See ya." I turned and walked away.

Weirdo.

I rounded the corner and practically sprinted down the

hallway to the back entrance, a smattering of rose petals flaking off from the poor bouquet in my hand. But just before slamming open the door, I skidded to a halt. Through its dirty windowpane, I saw Felix's blue jacket on the other side. But that's not all I saw: a perfectly manicured, red-nailed hand was pressed against the fabric. Another such hand emerged from his dark, curly locks.

Felix was kissing some girl.

I was frozen to the spot, but I can't say I felt anything in particular. I mean, I guess I was in shock: Here was this guy, making out with this other girl, not even half an hour after groping me. I wasn't angry, weirdly. I guess I was just dumbfounded, unable to wrap my brain around what I was seeing.

Then their bodies shifted, and through the grime I could make out her face.

Jill? Like, Felix's *sister*?

At this, my stomach started to seize up again, and I sank against the cinder-block wall to my left.

Get a grip, get a grip, get a grip.

OK, so either the Peronis had a very bizarre and probably illegal way of saying "Great show, sibling!" or I was the most gullible human being on the planet. My mind raced—what had Brianna said at Friendly's? She said she knew lots of Jills at school, but no Jill Peroni.

Well, of course. Because Jill *Peroni* didn't exist.

Oh, crap. I was totally gonna puke again.

My head spinning with random thoughts, I stumbled my

way back toward the lobby, lurching from pink rose petal to pink rose petal.

Pink ribbons . . . red T-shirt . . . sick grandmother . . . perfect white teeth . . . what big ears you have . . . obsessed with greens . . .

I paused, holding myself up on a wall while the floor started pitching back and forth.

Midnight curfew . . . the bean he spilled . . . you want the occasional sweet . . . stupid cow.

In the lobby, the first thing I saw was Jimmy scolding his be-turbaned sister. "Stop it! Stop yelling at people—you nearly gave that old lady a heart attack!"

Stupid, stupid cow!

Then I saw Oliver hugging Kirby's dad—the redheaded man in the audience—with Oliver's dad standing right next to them, smiling.

The lights in the lobby suddenly seemed extra bright, shining hard onto the crowd, and a faint buzzing sound started to build. I saw Derek and Kirby walking toward me, but it seemed more like they were swimming.

And the last thing I remember seeing was Oliver's dad holding hands with Kirby's dad.

artha. Wake up."

I opened my eyes. Derek's face, full of concern, hovered above me.

"Wh-wh-what's—" I stammered.

Derek shushed me. "It's OK, it's OK. You fainted."

Kirby's head appeared next to Derek's.

"Where—"

"Bathroom," said Kirby. "You dropped just outside the boys' bathroom. No worries, we got you. You were only out for, like, three seconds."

I breathed deeply twice. Then—

"Oh, my God—Felix!" I spat, my body jerking up. "Oliver's dad . . ."

Kirby and Derek grabbed me by the shoulders and eased me back down on the tile floor.

"Relax!" Kirby commanded. "Relax."

I tried to calm myself by getting lost in his amazing green eyes. Then I snorted through another few deep breaths, and a tear made its way toward my right ear.

"Felix is—"

"An asshole," Derek said. "We know. When was the last time you ate something? Jenny told us you hurled backstage, and we were worried." He wiped at another tear on my left side.

When did I last eat? I couldn't remember. Or when did I last sleep?

"Did Felix just tell you he had a girlfriend?" Kirby asked sadly.

"No, I just saw . . . kissing" was all I could come out with.

"In the boys' dressing room, the way he talked about girls at the dress rehearsals, it was clear he was a dick," Derek said. "But we didn't know about the girlfriend until tonight, when she dropped by at intermission to give him flowers. He wasn't around, though."

Well, then. So I didn't witness some incest at the back entrance. I should have been glad, right? In my condition, I couldn't even tell. The ceiling tiles blurred with tears.

"Oliver actually punched him when he got back," Derek said, grinning.

"*What?*" I tried to sit up again, but they held me down, shushing me again.

"Yeah, Oliver was so pissed that Felix had played you," said Derek. "You can still see the bruise under Felix's makeup."

Ah. I supposed that explained the dimple flinch. And that probably meant that our shadow-dabbled rendezvous was Felix's last chance for hooking up with me, since I'd soon find out about the fight.

Oliver. My valiant, honor-defending Oliver.

"And the dads. Oliver's dad . . . ," I said, trailing off. Geez, what was *that* all about?

"Which one?" asked Kirby after a moment. "Bill or Greg?"

Uh, what?

"What do you mean?" I asked.

"Well, which of his dads?" Derek said. "Er—what were you trying to say?"

My brain was not computing. "Wait, he has two dads? Like, a dad and a stepdad?"

"Nooooo . . . he has two dads," said Kirby. "The same way Heather has two mommies. Did you hit your head when you fell?"

Two dads.

Oliver's parents were gay.

I groaned and covered my face with my hands. "Oh, my God. I am such an idiot."

Kirby and Derek exchanged a puzzled glance.

"I assumed that one of Oliver's dads," I said to Kirby, "was *your* dad."

Stunned silence.

"Um . . . I don't even know where to begin with that one," Derek finally said. "Is it because of Greg's hair?"

Kirby laughed. "I suppose gingers all look the same to you?" he asked me.

"I'll just shut up now," I said groggily. But I didn't. "Gay dads . . . gay son. That's a lot of gay in one family."

"Wait, did Oliver tell you his brother is gay?" Derek asked.

"No, I mean Oliver."

"*What?*" they said in unison.

Kirby laughed again. "I know I said before that everyone's gay, but I like to think of Oliver as the exception that proves the rule."

At this point, I could *not* have been more disoriented. Black was white, up was down, and gay was straight. I struggled, in vain, to make sense of it.

"But he started the GSA."

"Yeah, the Gay-*Straight* Alliance," said Kirby. "Which is the main reason I believe Oliver when he says he's straight. Although I'm sure his having two dads is not just a co-incidence."

Shit. On the drive to Lake Erie, Oliver had said that he had started the group because he wanted things to be more fair. *Like, for his dads*; they couldn't get married in Ohio.

His dad was worried that Oliver wasn't butch enough. Worried because of gay dads. How ridiculous, and his dad knows it.

Wait a minute. "But you said he dated some guy," I shot at Derek.

Derek was clearly perplexed. "I did? When?"

"When the—you know—at the playground. You said Oliver just broke up with some guy."

His confused expression suddenly melted into a smile. "Ohhhh, I know what you're thinking," he said. "Charlie."

"Yes! Charlie!"

It took me a second to see that both of them were laughing.

"What's so funny?"

"Charlie's a girl!" they cried in unison.

Somehow I managed to sink lower into the floor.

"Charlie's a girl?" I floundered. "But . . . her name's Charlie!"

"Yeah, that's pretty weird, huh, *Marty*?" said Kirby with a smirk.

Derek slapped his arm. "Her real name is Charleston, but everyone calls her Charlie."

Kirby shook his head. "She is such a jerk, though. Mean."

"Oh, Marty!" Derek clutched his own head in his hands. "I had no idea you thought Oliver was gay! He's been so into you the whole time! I mean, why do you think Oliver is even doing this play?"

Um, good question. I *thought* it was because he had gotten Derek involved.

"Oliver's had a huge crush on you ever since he first laid eyes on you," he continued. "And, well, he kinda thought you were together, after the date you two went on."

My head was reeling. "Date? What date?"

Derek reddened. "The day he got his license?" He looked to Kirby for support. "At least, that's what he called it."

Looking out at Lake Erie, holding hands with Oliver, leaning into him. There was no kissing, but it was way . . . intimate. It *was* a date. A great one.

My first date.

"I mean, he was always coming up with reasons to see you," Derek added. "The photo shoot, the Bollywood movie, the bowling trip, dinner at your house . . ."

Suddenly Xiang's head poked in through the door. "You

OK in there? I'm having trouble holding off a whole bunch of guys from coming in. And they kinda have a point, since they *did* just sit through a three-hour show."

"No, we're done. I'm OK," I said, raising myself up. Derek and Kirby didn't object this time and, instead, helped me to my feet.

"Your parents are looking for you, by the way," Xiang said after I passed her, unsteadily, at the doorway, and as five males urgently pushed their way into the bathroom. "Actually, I saw them looking for you before you fainted, so they don't know anything about this."

I paused and turned, touching Xiang lightly on the arm. "About yesterday . . ."

Her face tightened. "Whatever. Let's just find your parents and get you home."

But then she paused. "Not that you deserve to know this, but do you know what I heard earlier tonight? Oliver is totes in love with you! Didn't you tell me he was gay?"

So, folks, that's basically the story.

On Saturday morning I woke up a totally different human being. I was no longer a walking train wreck. Sunlight streaming onto my bed, I sat up to find that I had a whole new level of clarity about who I was, what I wanted, and what I was going to do. (Actually, it was more like 2:00 P.M.; unconscious from the moment I made contact with my bed the night before, I'd slept for a solid fourteen hours.)

I walked downstairs to find my parents reading the paper in the kitchen.

"Well, well. Sleeping Beauty awakes," said my dad.

"And I feel a million times better," I said cheerily, opening the cupboards and digging around, hoping to find cereal that didn't look like it came directly from a grain silo.

My parents exchanged a surprised look: *She speaks!*

"Could one of you guys please drive me to Jerry Hall a little early today?" I asked. "I want to get there by four. But before that, I need to go over to Jimmy's. Oh, and I'll ride my bike over to Xiang's, too."

My mother folded up her newspaper and put it down on the counter. "So you've patched things up with her?"

"Well, I hope to, anyway." I could tell my parents were

walking on eggshells, trying to keep me from sliding back into silent mode.

I settled on a box of organic granola-y stuff.

But my dad couldn't resist treading further: "So, ah, how are things with Oliver?"

I spun around, wide-eyed. "How did you know about *that*?"

My dad chuckled. "Look, we may be old fogies, but it doesn't take magical powers to see that the boy is smitten with you."

Oh, my God. The shame! Even *my parents* knew! I thought back to that horrible night weeks ago, when my parents had set up The Rules.

The Boy Rules.

The *Oliver* Rules.

My shoulders slumped. Oh, geez. I'd gotten it all wrong, hadn't I? Maybe my parents couldn't care less about Jimmy and Derek.

"Well, to be honest, things with Oliver are not great," I said carefully, popping open the cardboard box of the granola stuff. "There was a lot of misunderstanding. On my part. About a lot of things."

I ripped open the plastic bag inside the granola box. "It's one thing I hope to patch up today." I swept up the little granola bits that managed to get all over the counter. "Actually, there's a long list."

Then I grabbed a small handful of granola stuff and shoved it into my mouth.

Hmm, not bad!

"Martha! Use a bowl," Mom scolded me, getting up and pulling a spoon from the drawer. "And get some milk or yogurt. You're not an animal."

"Fiiiiiine," I mumbled, opening the fridge door.

"And get some orange juice," said my dad, who was turning back to the paper. "You need vitamins. You're looking too pale these days."

"Yeah, yeah . . ."

As I put together a proper breakfast—brunch?—I realized that things at home were going to be OK. Not perfect, maybe, but definitely OK. And I can live with OK.

My long list was one line shorter.

The leaves were changing, and the air was chilly, making each breath prickle pleasingly as I crunched my way through the woods. The light was angled low, catching the leaves as they trembled in the breeze, igniting their colors.

Every few steps, I would stop by a tree, pull out my scissors, and snip off a gray, worn ribbon.

Then I'd pull out my roll and tie a new, fluorescent pink one in its place.

I heard approaching footsteps, twigs snapping.

"Hey." Jimmy stood a few yards away.

"Hey," I said.

"Oh, yeah, I was thinking it's about time we got new ones," he said, indicating my ribbons.

"Yeah," I said, not quite sure what else to say.

"I mean, *we* don't need them," he continued, pushing some leaves into a mound with the side of his shoe. "But we might have to send other people on the trail."

"Like Derek," I said, and he looked up to meet my gaze.

"Or Oliver," he said.

Our breaths came out in tiny puffs.

"Or Xiang, or Kirby," I said.

Jimmy pulled an annoyed face. "*Hello,* I'm trying to create a moment here!" he whined, hand on hip. "Xiang and Kirby do not belong on that list. I like Derek, the way you like Oliver, and we're supposed to be all meaningful and poetic about letting them into our lives, *as represented* by this trail."

Oh, Jimmy.

"So just to be clear," I said, "you knew the whole time that Oliver was straight?"

He nodded, giggling. "I still can't believe you got that wrong! Right after we did the whole photo-shoot thing at the playground, you said he was super-cute, so I brought him around to your house—"

"What? Wait, you were thinking about me and him together . . . as early as *then*?"

"—but then you ended up making out with Felix at the first rehearsal, so I didn't think you were interested. At all."

"I can't even . . ." I shrugged helplessly. "But when did you figure out that I was Oliver's crush?"

"Derek told me while you were off driving around with Oliver on his birthday." Jimmy looked skyward and sighed.

"I *may or may not* have been complaining to Derek that you were getting all buddy-buddy with Oliver . . . and Derek couldn't help himself; he told me. He was about to *explode* from having to keep it secret."

As the Queen of Unkept Secrets, I couldn't really fault him.

"Anyway," he continued, "Derek figured that since you guys were on an actual date, it wasn't secret anymore."

"But you didn't say anything to me?"

"Well, I thought *you knew* it was a date and that you had decided to stop seeing Felix! It seemed like you had every-thing under control. You weren't exactly giving me updates on anything."

No, it's true: I wasn't telling him much at all. I sighed heavily and clumped over to a fallen tree trunk to sit. Jimmy walked over to join me, sidling right up next to me for warmth.

"Marty, Marty, Marty . . . " Jimmy's breath had the crisp eucalyptus smell of cough drops.

"You silly, stupid succotash," I said, leaning my head on his shoulder.

"Yes, my ridiculous Rapunzel," he said, patting my leg.

Oooh, good one.

After a minute of just sitting there and listening to the soft rattle of leaves in the breeze, Jimmy spoke again: "You know, a minute ago, you didn't correct me."

I lifted my head. "I didn't?"

"So you *do* like Oliver."

* * * * *

Ding-dong!

Click-click.

Creeeak.

This time it was Xiang's mother who answered the door, and she broke into a wide smile.

"Oh, Martha!" she said. "You sang so beautifully last night."

I lowered my head, giving her my best "Aww, shucks" smile. "Thanks. Is Xiang home?"

"Yes, upstairs. Her bedroom is right at the top."

This was the first time I'd ever actually been inside Xiang's house, since she always wanted to leave it. I climbed up the thick-carpeted steps and knocked on the first paneled door.

I heard an annoyed *"What?"* and then the door flew open.

"Oh. Marty. Um, hi," Xiang said, clearly caught off guard.

"May I come in?"

She paused for a second, then nodded, and I slowly walked in. Her bedroom was immaculate, all tasteful dark furniture and cream-colored walls, with a music stand set up in a corner. There was no sign that anyone under the age of thirty lived there.

"I can't believe I haven't been here before," I breathed admiringly.

"Yeah. Well," Xiang said, clearly uncertain how she should handle the situation—me.

"So the past couple days have been pretty intense, huh?" I said, stalling. Apologies don't come naturally to me.

She merely looked at me, not showing any emotion.

"OK, I'll just say it," I finally said. "I'm sorry. I'm really, really sorry."

Still no reaction.

"You were being a really good friend, and I . . . wasn't. I'm sorry."

More silence.

"Right. Look, I'm happy for you and Parker, and I was probably a little jealous that you seem to be totally happy and in control of everything, while I'm just . . . a mess."

I ran my finger along her polished desktop as a few more seconds ticked by. "And I've been really self-absorbed. I get that. And that's probably how I got into this whole mess in the first place."

Her window had a view of the sidewalk, where an old man shuffled along. "You were right that I wasn't ready to . . . do stuff . . . with Felix. And I'm sure you've heard about what a total jerk he is. But that still doesn't excuse anything. I shouldn't have sworn at you, and I should have just—"

"OK, can you shut up already?" I looked up to see her grinning at me, arms folded. "I'm just giving you a hard time! Jesus, everyone goes crazy a little sometimes. No big deal."

"It *is* a big deal," I said, relieved by her sudden transformation.

"Well, whatever, not to me," she replied dismissively. "I knew you were just going bonkers temporarily. But let's not do that again, OK?"

"Promise," I said.

"And now comes the fun part." She squinted and steepled her hands, drumming her fingertips.

"What do we do about Felix?"

I suppose you're thinking we planned an elaborate act of revenge against Felix. Drugged him, shaved his curly locks, and tattooed BITCH on his forehead, perhaps? Or arranged for something sharp and heavy to fall on him during the final performance?

Nope. I figured that doing anything would just have gotten us into trouble and made it seem like I cared. And I honestly *didn't* care; in fact, the only emotion I could muster in regard to him was relief. OK, maybe a touch of revulsion, too. His poor girlfriend.

I'd had enough drama. Plus, revenge would have been totally beneath the new me. (And I don't know *anything* about a recent anonymous e-mail to Holy Name's Jill Cavanaugh. Nope, nothing at all.)

To tell you the truth, not really retaliating was probably the best revenge of all. All throughout the last performance of the show, Felix was clearly paranoid that I had something planned. I had never seen him so insecure, painstakingly avoiding me and looking at me with abject terror, like I was pointing a loaded weapon at him. (Which, btw, really messed up the whole Big Bad Wolf/Little Red Riding Hood dynamic in the first act).

Of course, word had gotten around to the whole cast and crew about his girlfriend and his fight with Oliver, so no one would speak to him, not even Jenny McCafferty. Everyone was being extra nice to me, too, although they may have just been worried that I would spew chunks at any moment.

To Felix's credit, though, he *did* show up for the performance, as justifiably horrible as it must have been for him. I half hoped that he wouldn't show and perhaps Oliver would be sent in as his understudy.

Sigh. Oliver.

There is one final bit to the story.

Maria Kilkenny, it turns out, comes from a pretty fancy-schmancy family. She lives in a big modern house in Lakewood, perched atop a steep bluff along Lake Erie. There's a big deck facing the water, and the nighttime view from there is *unreal*: just the twinkly Cleveland skyline off in the distance to the right and a vast black emptiness directly ahead, the tiny whitecaps of waves winking in and out of existence near the shoreline. I can't even imagine how gorgeous it is in the daytime.

It was pretty cold out, so the Kilkennys had set out kerosene heat lamps on the deck and had left piles of fleece blankets on the random groupings of tables and chairs. Bowls of chips and salsa were scattered about, and towers of plastic cups were posted next to a small battalion of two-liter pop bottles. With strings of tiny lights wrapped around the balustrade and lit candles set out in glass vases, the whole space glowed, like a fancy wedding reception in a movie.

All the kids involved with the show were there after the

performance on Saturday—all except Felix, who managed to get out of costume and disappear before most people even reached the dressing rooms after curtain call. Some of the guys were at one side of the deck, seeing who could spit the farthest out toward the water. Jenny McCafferty was on the other side, telling a bunch of orchestra girls and Kate O'Day war stories from her time managing the spring play last year. They were laughing, genuinely laughing, at what Jenny was saying, and she was clearly in seventh heaven. Xiang, Parker, Jimmy, and Derek were playing a heated game of Hearts at one table, and I was nestled under a blanket at another, talking to Maria, Calliope, and Penelope, the girl who'd played the Baker's Wife, about theater-y stuff. (If you must know, about who played *Gypsy*'s Mama Rose best on Broadway. I still say Angela Lansbury.)

Out of the corner of my eye, I saw Oliver putting on his jacket in the kitchen.

"Hold that thought. I'll be back soon to *completely* disagree with you," I said to the girls, casting off my blanket and making my way inside.

Oliver and I still hadn't spoken since our blowout on Thursday. I'd awakened that morning (OK, yes, afternoon) resolved to make things right with him, but, considering how horribly I had treated him, it just hadn't felt right to start the reconciliation process with a text or a phone call. As much as I dreaded it, this had to be done in person.

I had asked my parents to bring me to the theater early because I'd hoped to catch Oliver alone. It turned out, however, that he was even better at avoiding me than Felix was. Every time I'd tried to make eye contact with Oliver during notes both before the show and during intermission, he'd looked away and busied himself with checking microphones or reviewing Jenny's extensive to-do lists. Throughout the show, I'd searched backstage, hoping to corner him somewhere (and inadvertently sending Felix scurrying off), but he'd always managed to duck away just before I could actually say something. He wouldn't talk to Derek or Jimmy, either.

But finally, this was my chance. By the time I had gotten to the kitchen, though, Oliver was already at the front door.

"Oliver, wait!" I called out. "Don't go yet!"

He paused, his hand on the doorknob, for just a moment. But then he turned the knob and went out.

"Oliver!" Goddammit. I hustled after him. "Stop! Please!"

He'd made it to his car by the time I caught up. It was parked along the street, close to where the pavement met the edge of the bluff, which dropped precipitously to the shoreline below.

"Please," I huffed, trying to catch my breath. He stood, holding the car keys, waiting, as the jagged crashing of waves measured off the long moment.

"What?" he said, not making eye contact. "What do you want?"

He didn't say it like a question; he said it like "Go away."

"Look, I know you're mad at me, and you have every right to be pissed," I started, tears already pooling in my eyes. The crying was involuntary and totally annoying; I wanted him to see that I was sorry, not for him to feel sorry for me.

"Mad? I'm not mad," he said brusquely.

"I'm trying to apologize," I insisted, my voice breaking. The wind whipped my hair around my head, and my whole body began to tremble with nerves.

"I'm not mad," he repeated, taking a step away and *actually turning his back* to me.

"Of *course* you are!" I cried. "Come on, Oliver, you won't even look at me!"

I watched the back of his head shake back and forth. "Marty, I'm not mad," he said quietly, so I could barely hear him over the waves and the wind.

Then he slowly turned around and finally met my gaze. He swallowed and took a breath, and I realized he was close to tears, too.

He whispered, "I'm just fucking humiliated."

Yeesh. I'd only ever heard Oliver swear once before.

And I'd never seen him look so self-conscious, so vulnerable, so . . . sad. I mean, this wasn't him. None of this was the Oliver I knew.

I tried to say something, but it seemed that my heart had suddenly lodged itself in my throat. I swallowed hard, my whole body still vibrating.

And I don't know where this instinct came from, but instead of blurting something out, I grabbed the back of Oliver's neck and went in for a kiss.

I mean, I had made out with Felix, obviously, so it's not

like kissing was brand-new. But Felix generally initiated the kissing, pushing his face into mine, so I always knew he was up for it. This was totally different: Oliver looked like he could slug me at any moment, and I *promise*, I wasn't even planning to kiss him.

But, for some totally inexplicable reason, I just engaged autopilot and violated his personal space.

And, thank heavens, it turned out to be the right thing to do. Oliver's body jerked a bit upon contact, but it wasn't long before he relaxed and eased into a prolonged smooch.

When I came up for air, cheeks totally wet by this point (Hey, now—by my tears! We're not *dogs*), I held his head with both hands, forcing him to look directly into my eyes.

"I. Am. So. Sorry. This was totally my disaster, not yours. You have *nothing* to be embarrassed about."

He smiled wide, his puppy brown eyes crinkling at the edges. "Hmm. Not so sure about that. I mean, initially I just thought I was being rejected for some creep."

I felt a stab.

"Now, don't get me wrong, that's pretty bad," he continued. "But then I realized I had misread a girl's signals to the point where I thought I was on a date—at the same time that she thought I was gay. And the fact that the misunderstanding didn't get cleared up *during the course of the date*? Yeah, you know, that's not something I'm particularly proud of."

I returned his smile. "Well, in your case, it wasn't really as bad as that, since it wasn't just any girl."

"I suppose she does have her charms . . ."

"No, silly, not in *that* way," I said, finally relaxing a bit and giggling, slapping his chest lightly. "Your little misunderstanding wasn't as bad as you say, because the girl in question was one hundred percent beyond clueless. The whole making-wild-assumptions thing. Like, I still can't believe I somehow thought your dad was holding hands with Kirby's dad."

He nodded slowly. "Yeah, I have to admit, when Kirby told me that one . . ."

"*And* this girl couldn't identify a total jerk." I kicked at the ground.

He chuckled. "'*Even flowers have their dangers,*' huh?"

A last puzzle piece clicked into place. The card! "Oh, my God. That card was from you, wasn't it?"

Seeing my surprise, he reddened a bit. "I didn't really know what else to do," he mumbled. "You didn't want to hear it from me, so I figured a bit of anonymous advice never hurt anyone . . ."

I let this sink in for a moment, still clutching Oliver's waist, and he mine. I thought about how Xiang had described her relationship with Parker as natural . . . *comfortable.*

I think I understood that now.

Thinking back, I was attracted to the *idea* of being with Felix more than actually being with him. Or I didn't know what I wanted, really. I was so busy trying to be the person I thought he might like that I didn't spend a whole lot of energy getting to know him. (Obviously.)

But when I'm hanging out with Oliver, I know he likes me for the person I already am (even now, despite everything!). And *I* like me when I'm around him.

More to the point, I *really* like who Oliver is. He's just so great, and he makes me want to be better.

(And now I think he's even cuter than Felix ever was.) ;-)

"So, anyway," I continued, fingering a belt loop on his jeans. "This girl needs to make it right with you. She wants to. Somehow."

"Well," Oliver said, straightening up, "fortunately, I am what you might call an idea man."

He drew me closer. As our foreheads touched, I couldn't help but note the contrast with my last encounter with Felix. Instead of rising panic, I felt nothing but desire bubbling up.

"In fact," he continued, his lips brushing up against mine, "I have a number of suggestions. Starting with—"

Well. You can probably guess the rest.

Linas Alsenas has spent—OK, *spends*—way too much time singing show tunes to himself in the mirror. He has written several books for children and young adults, including *Gay America* and *The Princess of 8th Street*. Raised in a suburb of Cleveland, Ohio, Linas now lives in London with his husband and works at a children's book publisher.